The Strength of the Hills

Elswyth Thane

CHRISTIAN HERALD HOUSE

Chappaqua, New York

THE STRENGTH OF THE HILLS, without the postscript in this edition, was originally published as RELUCTANT FARMER by Duell, Sloane and Pearce, New York in 1950.

ISBN: 0-915684-06-3

LIBRARY OF CONGRESS CATALOG CARD NUMBER: 75-45861

To

Elmer La Flamme

I will lift up mine eyes unto the hills, from whence cometh my help. PSALM 121:1

Honour and majesty are before him: strength and beauty are in his sanctuary. PSALM 96:6

Here among the beautiful hills of Vermont, spirit and grace are alive on the earth. The peaceful passage of days sometimes reminds me of a day in the autumn of 1939 when the war was only a few weeks old, and England was under blackout and air raid precautions ruled. I had accompanied a young English girl from London to join her family at Cheltenham, a dreaming town in the Gloucestershire hills. As an American guest at a comfortable hotel there, I was touched and flattered to be adopted as a friend by a beautiful old lady, frail but indomitable, who had already lived through the 1914 war, and having lost her husband was left quite alone in the midst of a new war. Her concern was all for me, the stranger, with a hazardous journey home still ahead of me. In the kindness of her heart she invited me to take tea with her in her own room "at the top of the house," where she had an electric kettle and made her own teas, with little cakes from the bakery. Together we climbed two flights of stairs, and I at once exclaimed with pleasure at the view from her generous window, which looked towards the gentle rolling heights of the green Cotswolds. Her smile was sweet and brave. "Ah, yes," she agreed, and added quietly, " 'I lift up mine eyes to the hills. . . .' "

1.

THERE MUST BE AN easier way to paint wooden sap buckets.

Either you squat on a potato crate with the bucket on the floor of the barn loft between your knees—which soon requires a loosening of the belt and makes the back of your neck ache. Or you rest the bucket on the crate and bend over it, which is very hard on the middle of the back. Or you contrive some sort of bench, like a sawhorse, which wobbles, and stand up to it. And that's not comfortable either, for long.

When the insides have dried and you come to do the outsides it's even worse. You can put the bucket on the crate and kneel beside it and paint half way down. Then you must turn it over and paint the bottom and up to where you left off. And then how do you move it? Or, the inside being thoroughly dry, you can wear the bucket on your left hand like an oversize mitt and twirl it slowly as you paint, and pretty soon your left arm drops off.

It was a Sunday late in October and I had done the insides of thirty-five buckets, working all by myself in the barn loft. To get to them I had ascended from an overturned bucket on the floor to a stack of fertilizer bags piled against the outer wall of the stalls, and hoisted myself from there to the loft and slung my ski jacket over the beam so I wouldn't crack my skull every time I carried a finished bucket to the rows at the other end of the loft. Thirty-five buckets—new, glossy white on the inside, still weathered and dull on the outside. They looked very nice in the neat perpendicular triangular pattern they form when set alternately on the edges of the row below. But they had made no hole at all in the towering columns of unpainted buckets lodged one inside the other and stacked upside down which still had to be done.

Even though the barn faces west and the sunset pours through its open doors, the golden light was fading fast and its warmth was gone at the early end of the northern day. I lowered myself rather stiffly over the fertilizer bags and stepped out into the yard. And standing there in the reddening glow which promised more perfect weather to come, I was suddenly caught by an exultation that I had not often experienced even in what we think of now as the old, carefree days before the war, not even back in my never very lighthearted childhood before the Other War, when the world was young and life was simple and the Germans stayed in the geography books.

It was the year 1947—but for a few dazzling, unexpected moments I didn't care, and nothing loomed, and all was joy, because the land under my feet was mine, in at least one direction towards the rising horizon of the westward hill the land as far as anyone could see was mine, timber, water, and meadow, and I was the land's, and together we accomplished and produced, and it was give and take, turn about, and we were grateful each to the other, and we belonged. Yet I was not identified with the place by any chain of past generations who had loved it too and served it and been kept by it. I had bought it, rather impulsively, in rather recent years. But I had bought it with money I had earned myself, which perhaps in a way made it even more my own than if I had just sat still and inherited it.

When the sun goes down on the farm it sinks abruptly behind the hill which shelters the house set facing the downward slope to the town road and a deep ravine and another hill, over which the sun arrives in the morning with similar suddenness. Before it goes it prints the sharp shadows of the hill's evergreens and maples on the hayfields in front of the house. Just as the tops of the shadow-trees touch the stone wall at the bottom of the field the sun is gone from our side, and all shadows merge into a general twilight, and only the upward slope of the opposite hill, with the Aldriches' cows coming home along the skyline, still lies in brilliant light. I stood there, revolving slowly, knowing it had never looked so lovely, and that I had never been so aware.

The blinding flash of feeling, of sentiment, if the abused word must be used, was gone in the space of a few quickened heartbeats. But the memory of it has returned again and again —just that particular minute out of a whole autumn, with the shadows long at my feet and the late pink light creeping away across the fields—just that one special evening in the barnyard when swift, unreasoning contentment, all the brighter for being brief, blotted out the Atomic Age.

It was one of those peaks of acute perception, sometimes hardly recognized until after they are gone, which stud an eventful life like milestones. There was a night between the wars when I came up the English Channel towards Plymouth on the bridge of a transatlantic liner, and talked in the dark to an unknown officer on the dog-watch whose face I never saw, but through whose quiet voice and casual-seeming phrases I glimpsed the breadth and courage and calm and duty and devotion of the British merchant marine; there was an afternoon at Glastonbury when I stood within the sun-drenched ruins on the velvet lawns and felt in the pit of my own stomach, as the martyred Abbot must have felt in his, the terror and the desolation and the despair which the Reformation brought to the shrine; there was the day I first saw the Tudor manor house of Compton Wynyates from the untravelled road which curves above it—and an evening in a Hertfordshire pub as the salty locals mellowed towards closing time—and the moment I first realized that air-raid trenches were being dug in a London park—and another night at sea on the voyage home with the world at war again and the Atlantic full of submarines, when I stood at the rail and watched the American flag fluttering at the masthead in a searchlight. . . . You can count them on your fingers, in the end, but this was one of them—this swift knowledge of the land as mother earth.

The magic light was fading fast, and the air had turned quite chilly. I closed the heavy sliding doors to the barn, the left-hand one of which always takes all the pull there is in my un-accustomed back, and crossed the yard and the lawn to the silent, dusky house. Sunday is a day, the only day, when nothing ever happens. The man who works on the place doesn't come, the milk and eggs don't come, there is no deilvery of groceries, bottled gas, or fuel oil. The third of a mile of stony road which leads up to the house from the mail-box is empty all day. It is the last word in blissful solitude, linked of course by the telephone to what is still laughingly called civilization.

The lock of the woodshed door went home behind me. My drawbridge was up. A finger on the kitchen light switch brought the prompt, obedient hum of the Kohler plant in its own small house beyond the choke cherry hedge, and the kitchen was bright with shaded bulbs. The little brown bird who would be my only companion that night had gone to bed on his branch in the window above the sink. There was nothing more to make fast, no need to draw blinds or shield lights. The place was my own, secure, and snug, and—in an uneasy world—as safe as any place could be. Food in abundance was in the white refrigerator and on the pantry shelves. Fuel for the winter, both wood and oil, was already laid in and paid for. The bird and I were equipped for a siege if need be, and he at least knew a happy confidence in a benign future.

The brief wave of ecstasy had passed, perhaps forever, but a deep sense of well-being remained as I set about getting my solitary supper. For these few days Che-Wee-the-bird and I were alone in our castle. My husband was in New York, my mother had gone away for a visit. Che-Wee and I had not the grace to miss either one of them. We mightn't like it forever, mind you, but we were doing all right. If we got scared we had the telephone, but we never got scared, even when the wind blew. And anyway we had a couple of guns. Besides the .22 we had the Marster's Luger and a clip full of cartridges. Neither of us had ever fired it, but he had, and we knew it went off with a wonderful bang. The only prowlers here were the deer, who apparently sometimes came and sat on the porch at night. And of course the things in the walls, and sometimes things in the attic which sounded rather like elephants, but we were used to those, and when the insulation went in they would go. Che-Wee slept in his cage in the middle of one of the guest-room beds where the window wasn't open. (The only use he ever makes of a cage is at night and for travelling. Each evening he has to be picked up and set on the perch inside it, so he

7

will be safe from mice and drafts, and we know where he is in the morning.) I went to bed almost as early in my room across the passage with a stack of books on the bedside table and read and read and read.

When we woke up on a Sunday like this one, I went downstairs in a dressing-gown and fixed a tray with orange-juice, tea, and toast and marmalade, and ran out to the end of the porch for a handful of blue-grass and chickweed with the dew still on them, for Che-Wee. Then I hooked open the door of his cage and got back into bed with the tray. He knew where to find me, and we breakfasted together at leisure, with some argument over how much marmalade was good for him, and he would then retire to the nearest lampshade to do his feathers while I picked up the book I had laid down when sleep overtook me the night before.

And that is the way this book began to be written.

2.

W<small>E</small> HAVE NEVER GIVEN
the place a name, and it cannot rightfully be called a farm because it has no livestock. Yet. It is simply the Place, as though
there was nowhere else we could possibly mean when we
speak of it, and the last thing I ever expected to do was to
write a book about it, so I must apologize to all the people
with whom I have been a bit brusque when they innocently
suggested such a thing. But it always seemed to me that Fred-
eric Van de Water had covered the ground thoroughly and
delightfully, and he has had a lot of followers and imitators
far less delightful. Every time I read another account of how
some lighthearted nitwit bought a ramshackle barn in a wilder-

ness just for laughs and turned it into a milk-and-honey paradise—and a book—I got madder. And as everyone knows,
books by and about people who discovered the country and
promptly rolled in it began a few years ago to come faster than
you could read them, until they finally reached a sort of apoth-
eosis in the pitiless parody enshrined in Craft-Cooke's *Miss
Allick*. They were usually pretty coy and self-conscious, as
autobiography has a fatal tendency to be, especially in the
hands of the inexperienced writer. They were likely to have
silly names for everybody to hide behind, and were full of
patronizing stories about the local yokels and dressed-up drol-
leries of dialect which mostly rang very false. And I would
thank God audibly that we hadn't got a funny gardener and
that the efficient village store delivered a weekly grocery order
in a tidy Chevvy truck, so I didn't hear any cracker-barrel wit
when I did the marketing—by telephone. Besides, we didn't
have any animals on our place, and you can't write books
about country houses without pets.

Ours was bought early in the war—the most recent war—
as a summer home where my mother could grow some flowers
and where Will and I could work peacefully on manuscripts
and take walks and watch birds and have time to read aloud in
front of a log fire. It would fill in, we thought, while the war
was on and I couldn't get back to England to work in the British Museum library—I had begun a job on the youth of
Charles II before September, 1939—and Will's expeditions
were also necessarily curtailed. Our Bermuda house was gone
with the wind, after six happy years of remodelling and plan-
ning, swallowed up into the American air base. But you
couldn't easily get to and from Bermuda during the war anyway. I had been ill and war-time New York was exhausting,
and I needed extra rest and mild exercise.

As soon as we bought it we went so far as to put in a coal furnace for chilly weather, and a whopping fireplace for just cheer, and added a big insulated study in the attic. The house had never been wired, but we thought that with the long northern summer days we wouldn't mind lamps. The plumbing was all right, though the bathroom opened off the dining-room downstairs, and the bedrooms were all upstairs. There was a nice guest-room, but house guests would have to make their own beds and maybe wipe dishes. We had no room to accommodate our black maid from New York even if we had wanted to bring her, and female local help was invisible.

That, my dears, was the autumn of 1942. And here we are in 1949 with a winter-tight, fully electrified, year-round establishment, and here I am with a book about it. I am still surprised.

One of those evenings when Che-Wee and I were alone here, Will rang up from New York for a chat, and said among other bits of news that he was sending me the book Roy Chapman Andrews had just had published about their country place in Connecticut. And I said, "Oh, Lord, Roy *too?*" and Will said (Humorously, as the stage directions always put it) "Why don't *you* do one?" and I replied "Yah!" rudely and forgot about it.

Roy's book arrived the next day in its nice green jacket and I opened it with what the first Theodore Roosevelt used to call quarrelsome interest, because we had seen Roy's place in its early stages before they prettied it up and went in for bird-dogs and trap shooting. I had begun to read it that Saturday evening in bed. I read quite a lot of it before I turned out the light, disappointed that he had omitted the story about the time their white Persian cat Jitters went under the car and got black grease on its back and *somebody* had the bright idea of cleaning it off with Carbona. Of course the fluid smarted like sin, and Will and I lay on beach-mats on the lawn beneath the open bathroom window and shook with laughter at the uninhibited family brawl which ensued while they frantically tried to remove the sting of the Carbona from the cat's skin in a tub full of warm soap suds, and the cat told them exactly what it thought of them, and the question of *whose* idea it had been was threshed out. . . .

When I woke at the customary too-early-for-Sunday hour, though no alarm had rung, I went down to the kitchen and made the breakfast tray and returned to bed and Roy's book. About eleven a.m. I came to the last page. It was a nice warm day for painting sap buckets, but I lay there and thought, until a persistent clinking sound suggested that Che-Wee was up to something, and I raised my voice at him. Silence. Then, cautiously, the sound again. It seemed to come from the bureau, where a pile of clean clothes obscured my view from the near end. I yelled at him again, and his head showed over the top of the clothes, as he stood very tall to see me—"Hunh?" was the general effect. I knew then what the sound was. He was picking at the nose-pieces of my Oxford reading-glasses, which always have to be defended from him because his stout finch beak is strong enough to do real damage. He likes to drag them around by the black cord too, and drop them over the edges of things, when he gets a chance. "Stop it!" I told him. "Get out of there!" He flew up guiltily on to the top of the open closet door and wiped his bill, first on one side of him and then on the other, like dusting off his hands. *I* wasn't doin' nothin', the gesture always implies.

I lay there thinking of the odd way Will's life and Roy's had of repeating on them. Two men as different as red from green —both nice colors—but the similarity of externals recurred, one way and another. When we were first at Roy's Connecticut house years ago we got slightly bitten even then with the idea of having a little country place like that ourselves—nearer than Bermuda—for summer week-ends. They drove us over to look at a neighboring farm rumored to be for sale, which would never have done for us. But we did talk about it then. Because of Will's permanent preoccupation with the tropics, the idea took deeper root with me than with him, but we still had Bermuda then, and I always went to England in the summer.

Nevertheless, the seed was sown on that visit, when Roy and Billie still thought they had just a summer place too. We were rather surprised and sorry when they more or less retired into it and turned it into a year round residence. And now look. Of course we aren't living here the whole time ourselves. Not yet. No wedded pair of black guardian angels from Virginia have appeared to cook and run the house for us, but we have Elmer. No bird-dogs nor Persian cats here, just an orphan purple finch in his fifth year and outgrowing the book he has already badgered me into writing about him. No shooting parties nor dry fly fishing. Just a couple of second-hand tractors and a mowing-machine and a sugar-bush for us. But still—

This is your fault, Roy, you were the last straw. Now *I'll* tell one.

3.

BECAUSE I AM STILL
convinced that there have been too many I-Bought-a-Barn
books, I am not going into any laughable details about how we
searched for and found this house in the southern Vermont
hills. We didn't search long, we didn't give a hoot about a barn,
and we didn't meet any quaint characters while we were looking. It came of a normal week-end visit to the Van de Waters
made in connection with a book I was writing at the time. A
real estate agent came to dinner, a friend of theirs. I was in love
with the countryside at first sight, as everyone is, and I thought
it would be nice to have a house there, although I already had

a cottage on the Maine coast that I was fed up with because it was too small and too far from New York. One thing led to another, and they showed me a few places which were available but which for one reason or another weren't suited to our still very nebulous needs, and I went away. A little later they telephoned that they had found the right thing for me and I dashed back to look at it, and wanted it. Only a few days after that Will returned from Venezuela and was rushed up to Vermont for another week-end to see what *he* thought, and we bought it.

Things weren't actually quite as simple as that sounds, but it's near enough.

This was no house of our dreams, because we hadn't any, unless it was the one in Bermuda on which we had spent so much money and so many plans, all lost because of Hitler. We hadn't much money left to put into this one, and it took both of us, pooling what we could spare, to get it. Will was big about that, as his first sight of it was on a dreary autumn day with the leaves down and the shutters up, deserted by the "summer people" who had owned it for several years since it had ceased to be a productive farm, and naturally he couldn't see much in it. I had first met it in sunshine and when it was inhabited—stretching the word, for its owners spent only a few weeks in it each year. It did look pretty hopeless inside. Except for the four bedrooms, which had just been done over even to new wallpaper, and the kitchen, it was furnished with leftovers and near-antiques, badly arranged, but all included in the purchase price. There was a bathroom, and there was what seemed to be good kitchen equipment for a house without electricity, such as a new white enamel sink, wood-burning range, and ice-box. We could use the house for a while pretty much as it was, and since the contents of the Maine cottage would not have been adequate to furnish it from scratch this was a certain advantage in the beginning, though to my eyes the rooms all begged for drastic changes and elimination.

The water supply was a gravity spring, too far back in the woods to be visited that day, but famous for never running dry. The big red barn was in apparent repair, with a new slate roof, and unlike most barns did not obstruct the view, which ran round three sides of the horizon with the hillside rising on the fourth side behind the house. There was a third of a mile of dead-end road between the house and the town road which led to the hard-top which led to the village two miles away. The nearest neighbor was a farmer a mile in the other direction, his grey unpainted barn just visible on a turn of the road and his rolling hayfields beautifying the middle distance.

We laughed when they said a-hundred-and-eighty-acres-more-or-less went with the house. We thought ten would have been ample. They explained that land like that didn't cost much, it was the buildings we were paying for. Old sugar and wood roads, much overgrown, ran up the hill and branched out and lost themselves in the neglected woods, which were mainly hard maple and evergreens. On the far side of a grassy knoll behind the house and not visible from its windows stood a sugar-house full of neglected equipment and stacks of wooden buckets. They said that once you could set fifteen hundred buckets, but it would cost a good deal to put the apparatus into working order again, the way it had been treated. Two trout brooks formed a sort of triangle on the land, with the house and barn near the apex and front line, which was the unpaved town road. Haystack Mountain, the highest point hereabouts, overlooked us benignly from the north. We were twenty-two hundred feet up.

Well, we bought it, without an awful lot of enthusiasm, as

I look back. We remained conscious of the comforting fact that we could always get our money out of it, at that price. Make us an offer now. Any offer. The answer is No.

An outsize brick fireplace in the living-room and a furnace were to go in at once under the supervision of the agent, while we returned to New York, and two thirds of the attic space above the woodshed was to be insulated, floored with matched boards, and lined with wallboard to make a big study, with three southward windows. This was where I would work, at a big old dining-room table to be sent down from Maine, and from here the telephone—a seven-party line—could not even be heard to ring. (Of course that didn't last. I had an extension put in upstairs.)

I was able to sell the Maine cottage unfurnished, at short notice and a small loss, and had its contents sent to Vermont by truck. At Thanksgiving time, when the work on the house was supposed to be finished, we dispatched a truck load from New York too, and Mother and I came up to unpack and settle in so that everything would be ready in the spring. Because the head of the family isn't a handy man with a hammer and a pair of pliers, and hates cold weather, and we weren't sure how the heating system was going to work, he was let off that trip and a good thing too. The new furnace burned coal. And how. We either roasted or it went nearly out and had to be coaxed with our precious store of wood belonging to the kitchen stove which was all we had to cook on. There was some knack to the furnace which we never learned.

The new fireplace had been made of the last of a scarce local supply of antique red brick and looked as though it had grown there when the house was built, as we had hoped it would. It was set into plain ivory-painted panelling which matched the other woodwork in the living-room, with a thick, unadorned plank mantel shelf. But the workmen had not quite finished with it when they departed to give us possession for the duration of our stay, and while it would burn logs it leaked a savage blast of cold air all around the edges where the panelling met the brickwork, until we stuffed the crack with crumpled newspaper, later replaced by a neat putty job.

There was a pile of old cut wood in the woodshed which adjoined the kitchen. It was too short for any fireplace but we used it anyhow. It was also too long for the handsome white enamel stove, which had an abnormally small fire-box, and the problem of what to burn there was only solved by getting in a village boy to split and cut our wood to fit. The stove went out every night, regularly, even if assisted with coal. As the hot-water-tank in the bathroom was hitched to it, and no fire could be got hot enough to reach the water, we never had hot baths. The tub was just an ornament in the bathroom, it had never so far as we could see been of any practical use. Even dishwater had to be brought to an adequate temperature in tea-kettles, and I like lots of dishwater and it has to be hot.

When the large maple table was removed from the center of the long living-room where we found it and placed in a corner where it had a window on each side of it, and when the easy Lawson furniture from Maine was introduced in place of Great-Aunt-Emma's upright Victorian sofa and long-legged unyielding mahogany armchairs, it began to look more like home to me. I am not able to appreciate old furniture just because it is old, if it is ugly and uncomfortable too. During those summers in England before the war began I went to a good deal of trouble to see the insides of famous old houses, sometimes by invitation and sometimes on the days when the public is permitted to pay sixpence to view, and in a few cases I was chilled to the bone by their excessively period décor, more cheerless than museums yet heroically lived in by the spartan owners. While at others, like Hatfield and Bradenham, chintz-covered overstuffed sofas and armchairs in which it was possible to lounge in the modern manner, or at least to lean back, were gathered hospitably around the hearths and bay windows and did no artistic violence to adjacent linenfold panelling or Tudor oak, or to the Restoration chairs on whose high backs the little carven walnut hands have been presenting for nearly three hundred years a miniature carven crown. It need not be wholly Philistine to wish to be at ease while you drink your afternoon tea.

There seemed to be millions of cartons to unpack during that first Thanksgiving time stay, many of them containing nothing but books—books I had had before I was married, books a recently widowed godmother had donated from her own shelves to the cottage, and a lot more that were just in the way in New York, or that we hoped to find leisure here to read again some day. Will thus bestowed upon me his entire sets of Chesterton, Wells, Conrad and the like, which left room on the New York shelves for our more recent purchases piling up on tables and even on the floor as they carried on their mysterious monthly multiplication. He points out that when he removes one book from a shelf the others maliciously spread themselves to fill the hole before another can be inserted, and we even entertain the idea that our library has pups when our backs are turned. It stands to reason that we couldn't afford to buy all the books we seem to own, but they must come from somewhere, and we don't approve of stealing so it isn't that.

I had my own set of Kipling, so he lives in both houses simultaneously, and I won the best edition of the Britannica because it was getting shabby. Certain reference books have had to be acquired in triplicate, so that they can be left in the country house as well as in each of our work rooms in New York. The same boy who chopped wood put up some plain pine shelves in addition to some knocked down bookcase material which had come with the cartons, and we filled them as fast as the boxes were opened, hardly waiting for the paint to dry, else we couldn't have found room to sit down. There are now bookshelves in every room in the house and they are all full. Because there was no time to sort things as we unpacked, or we should never have got anywhere, I am still vague about where certain items have come to rest, though by now most of the authors have had all their volumes assembled on the same shelf.

The downstairs bathroom, in a house without an electric switch in it, was infuriating to a degree where I was heard to declare that by the time you got into a dressing-gown and slippers and took a flashlight and felt your way downstairs in a cold house with the furnace banked for the night, you might as well go all the way outside and down a path to a privy. There was no running water upstairs. If you didn't think to brush your teeth before you went up to bed you were out of luck. If you forgot to carry up a glass of water in your fist you went thirsty or you went back downstairs.

In Vermont the November days are very short, and during that first stay we lived in a peering fumble of exasperation. The charming Aladdin lamps with big parchment shades gave out a deceptively white and steady light, but to read or sew by it proved that it just wasn't *light*. So then you turned them up too high and the mantels caught fire and smoked the chimneys and the ceiling before you knew where you were. The ordinary kerosene lamps upstairs were a misery and a hazard. We are a family that likes to read in bed. As for the cleaning and filling of oil lamps for a nine-room house which we wanted to live all over, I won't dwell on it.

But there is a thrill about first arranging your belongings in a place of your own. And the only way to find out what you lack is to do without it. So we returned to New York before Christmas with a long list and a feeling of some satisfaction. Before we went we watched the snow line creep down the mountain towards us till big white flakes were beating against our windows.

The first summer we spent in the house was one of strict economy, after the essential expenditures already made. I had recently bought some new linen and bedding for the cottage in Maine, but that supply was not sufficient for a larger house. To equip ourselves with sheets, blankets, eiderdowns, bed-spreads, bureau scarves, and towels and towels and towels, all new, and now that the war-time shortages were beginning, was quite an item. My own big spool bedstead and its new mattress had been transplanted from Maine to Vermont, and the furniture bought with the house included three new maple bedroom suites with Simmons mattresses and down pillows, which were about the only part of its contents I could make any permanent use of.

I had chosen new wallpaper for all the downstairs rooms, and we began on that at once, as I had learned in Maine that anybody can put on wallpaper. Even Hitler. We did the living-room first, a wall at a time, because I simply couldn't bear looking at what was there. My sunny new landscape paper had a general background tone of deep cream and apricot, more suitable to a room with windows on the north and east than the cold oyster-grey-cum-brick-red pseudo-*toile* design which it replaced. But we concentrated mostly outside the house, on starting a vegetable garden and watching to see

21

what would develop in the flower-bed which ran down one side of the front lawn where three matched maple trees stood in a guardian row. Peonies, delphiniums, hollyhocks, monarda, phlox, and other perennial standbys appeared in due course, all in need of transplanting or division which trebled the supply and required more ground opened up, so we dug borders to a depth of two feet in front of the low grey stone walls which edged the lawns all round the house.

During our first Thanksgiving time stay, the Coopers had come to call on us, our neighbors from the next farm. It was deer-hunting week and they arrived picturesquely on foot across the hayfield wearing boots and bright jackets and with a rifle under his arm—just in case. They came out of kindness, to see if there was anything they could do to help us settle in, and we arranged to get our milk and eggs three times a week from them, and he agreed to bring over his team in the spring and plough and harrow a level patch below the house where we could plant peas and potatoes and corn. We thought the first time they set foot in the house that they were dears, and we still think so. To say we couldn't do without them is futile, but we should hate to try.

Setting down any sort of coherent record of what I did and thought and felt with regard to the place during those early years is difficult. It was a very casual undertaking in the beginning, an experiment which we hoped wouldn't cost too much; the war news was bad and I was much preoccupied. I have had cause once before, when I came to write a book about my twelve pre-war summers in England, to regret that I have always been too prudent, or too busy, or too self-conscious to keep any sort of diary beyond an engagement calendar. For England I had only a capricious memory, too briefly trained in newspaper work for its own good, so that it highlighted in heartbreaking detail some happy unimportant episode and left a foggy patch over something which later proved to have been a crucial point. For this job I have only my account books, begun out of curiosity and to keep track of what went into the venture above the purchase price in case we ever wanted to set our own price on its sale.

Something had to be done about the hot water first of all, and so the people who had installed the furnace put in what they called a hod-a-day stove with a new tank set-up in the cellar. The little stove burned chestnut coal. When it burned. I spent most of my time bending over it feeding in handfuls of twigs and boxes of matches and screws of newspaper, trying to start it again. You were never sure in the morning if it had lived through the night, but you knew pretty well what to expect. The water in the tank might be still warm, but the stove would be cold. It was a bad way to start the day, keeping your temper—or losing it—over a lump of indifferent iron.

Ice for the nice white enamel refrigerator came by truck from the railroad town twenty miles away. Delivery was made three times a week, but the season was short, starting after we arrived and ending before we wanted to leave. We discussed kerosene refrigerators, and decided that a kerosene stove would be more to the point. The first summer we did without either one.

Canned food was now rationed, which made stocking up the pantry impossible. Nobody in the family drove a car, so we didn't own one, relying on the village taxi service for meeting trains and doing errands beyond the weekly delivery from the general store. Wild fruit in abundance grew all over our hillside, and a good crop of apples from our old neglected trees roused canning ambitions and we did what we could on the wood range with some success. But everything in the house would freeze solid during the winter, and some of the jars we shipped to New York arrived there broken, so we were a little damped on that.

Always town and city bred, except for holidays, I had never recognized in myself any particular urge back towards the soil, although I once wrote a book in which an English country house serenely absorbed the lives and fortunes of generations of its owners. While I was gathering my material for that book I rented a cottage near some friends in Buckinghamshire and made long drives looping out into the Cotswold country. It was the summer that Haile Selassie was at Geneva putting the case of Abyssinia before the League while the Italians dropped mustard-gas bombs on his native warriors, and I used to sit in my little living-room in the quiet evenings listening to the cultured periods of the delegates and the BBC commentators on the radio in a sort of fourth dimension of incredulous remoteness. And yet, even then, we knew it was the writing on the wall.

Living there in the Buckinghamshire cottage during the ripe summer months, I had the privilege of using whatever the garden produced which would not keep till the owners returned. And so for the first time I knew what it was to carry out a bowl and pick ripe red raspberries from the canes for my breakfast, and to gather roses with the dew still on them for the table—also to pick and cook the first green peas and new potatoes from the generous garden next door.

And even then, I had a dim sort of dream of owning a place in the country some day, and Will and I used to read the illustrated ads in the front of the English *Country Life—Choice residential property, lovely old world grounds—hard tennis court and parkland—wild-flower garden—small home farm*

—kitchen garden and paddocks—like wistful window-shoppers outside Tiffany's. I noticed in Buckinghamshire that country nights were calm and still and mysterious, and I saw what a full moon can do to fields and trees and a garden, and I experienced early mornings, which are wasted on city dwellers. I learned the importance of weather, which can be more or less ignored in town. And even then, along with the growing premonition of war, I had begun to feel an awareness of rural security and contentment, some of which went into the book where it belonged, as part of the job I was doing, and some took deep root in me, to emerge years later in New England.

I spent the months following the publication of that book confessing to disappointed inquirers that I had never known a house like Queen's Folly, which was a composite of a dozen old houses in the Cotswold Hills like Compton Wynyates and Stanway, Owlpen and Wroxton, and which had no existence beyond my novelist's imagination. I am now quite prepared to kill the first person to suggest Thane's Folly as a label for this still nameless dwelling.

When Starr Cooper had prepared the ground for the vegetable garden with his plough and harrow Mother and I did the rest ourselves, working with spading fork and rake and hoe and reckless enthusiasm, in very short shifts and yet overdoing it so that we had to lie down flat every so often. But we got things planted, a row at a time. It was much too much for us, when we weren't used to it, I know that now. But during the course of my background reading for the Williamsburg books I had to consume a lot of novels written before and during the first World War, and one of these by Berta Ruck was about a delicate young Englishwoman who became a Land Girl and built up a wonderful state of rugged health in no time at all by sheer grit and sweat, and I wanted to see if it would work for me. It didn't.

Nobody human can fail to feel proud when seeds he himself has planted with unaccustomed toil actually come up. The first radishes and lettuce from our garden tasted better than any I have ever eaten, not just because they were fresher. They were *mine*. Peas and potatoes followed, and even tomatoes. The thing began to grow on me. The first faint squirrel instinct to lay away provender for the winter was stirring inside me. It irked me that none of our surplus produce could be stored in the house. But for what? We wouldn't be here. By the time we returned in the spring it would be spoilt. But I wasn't quite happy somewhere when we had to give away extra potatoes and carrots and cabbages.

There was one crop to harvest, though. The people who sold us the place had promised that the hay could be sold standing each year for enough to pay the taxes, which were minute. The Coopers grew all the hay they needed, but they brought another farmer who did want it, and he laid the money on the table before he started cutting, which I liked him for. Bad weather delayed him—his horses had to be stabled in our barn while they worked here—when they finally went we had a plague of flies. One felt that having the hay cut was more trouble than it was worth, but I understood vaguely that hay ought to be cut every year for the sake of the land it grew on, and I was willing that the same arrangement should stand for the following summer. Besides, the red barn with its fragrant fresh load of loose hay looked and smelled cosy and farmlike.

The next year was a low one for me, financially, and almost nothing was done on the place except some repairs to the living-room ceiling which was coming down on account of the drying furnace heat, and to the spring, on the advice of the plumber. The clear, cold water (which I am told is specially soft for shaving-soap) flows from a rock face in dense woods on the far side of the brook, into a wooden tank sunk into the ground, with a generous, perpetual overflow. Cutting timber away from around the source is one good way to dry up a spring, and our site has been preserved so that it lies always in deep shade, and is well worth a rough scramble on a damp, almost obliterated path to admire. From the wooden storage tank the water is piped down—through too small a pipe, owing to some prehistoric economy—underground to the house. Luckily the pipe was at least laid deep enough not to freeze, but the wooden tank was old and had to be replaced. Some new window curtains and drapes—that apricot tone in the living-room wallpaper, which wouldn't go with any normal flowered cretonne, proved to be most expensive to match—and the simplest possible living-room rug; creamy landscape paper in the dining-room, strawberries on a white ground on the kitchen walls, and a three-burner oil stove were the extent of other additions and repairs indoors.

A succession of small boys was hired to keep the lawn more or less mowed with an ancient machine which we found in the woodshed and which always broke down, and they did other odd jobs about the grounds and garden. They were expensive for what they accomplished, and they came when they had nothing better to do, and they couldn't work if it was hot because they had to go swimming—*had* to, or drop dead—but with their aid we were enlarging the lawn where it ran out into hay around the edges, and the place had begun to look more lived in and cared for.

The third year saw the end of the lamps, which had kept me in continual dread of fire. I had the house wiring begun the minute I caught the money to pay for it, without waiting to close any deal with the source of supply. And so there we were, with lots of baseboard outlets in every room, and even some electric lamps bought, and no current within a mile or so. The company power line ran to the Coopers' farm, but by-passed this house because the owners at that time had not seen fit to take advantage of the installation. The extra third of a mile between the house and the town road left the company a loophole not to oblige me. They refused to follow the telephone line across country from the Coopers' farm, I could never discover why. They talked instead of bringing their poles up our road, bang in the middle of the view—if they could find any poles, that is. If I didn't want poles in my view I could have the line laid underground, at my own expense. Or I could go on using lamps, for all they cared. Anyway, there probably weren't any poles, on account of the war. And besides, they probably wouldn't get round to it till next year, or maybe the year after.

My personal war with the power company need not be gone into here. I have seldom been as angry as I was at their representative's attitude of studied indifference to my wishes or welfare. I should thank him, however. When I get really mad —it doesn't happen often enough, perhaps—something has to give somewhere.

I bought a light plant.

4.

THE IDEA OF A LIGHT
plant was slow to dawn on me as my experience with them
was limited to the ones used on Will's expeditions in Haiti and
Bermuda, and those apparently were not automatic. On Non-
such Island in Bermuda where he had a station during the Thirties when the bathysphere descents were being made, the light
plant lived in the one-time mortuary, which was a little white
cubicle down a path through a cedar grove towards the ceme-
tery, and each night before John Tee-Van went to bed he
would walk down and turn off the engine. There was always
a scramble by anybody who was not yet sleepy (often only
me) to get a kerosene lamp lighted before the electricity went

29

off, and thereafter you groped and squinted and lost things and a flashlight was your only hope.

When it was explained to me about fifteen years later in Vermont that there were light plants which turned themselves on and off with the first and last electric bulb in a house hundreds of feet away I perked up. And I have since learned that the Bermuda light plant *was* automatic, or could have been, and nobody concerned has yet given me a satisfactory answer as to *why* I read by a kerosene lamp every night down there—beyond a vague mumble about aquaria and refrigerators which used a lot of current, etc. etc. etc. . . .

There was a world war on now, but I began my own campaign about a light plant, and the obliging man who had wired the house finally dug up a second-hand Onan at a figure which did not seem to me excessive in the mood I was in. Its radiator was about the size of an old-fashioned Ford's, and the rest of it was bobtailed and unimpressive and a rusty green, but they swore it would make electric light and I cheerfully wrote out a check. It would be too noisy to go in the woodshed or the cellar, and the barn was too far away—or something—so it was finally installed in the dilapidated chicken-house which stood fifty yards behind the main house screened by a choke cherry thicket. The floor was pretty well gone, and some of the windows were broken, but they boarded up one end of it, put on tar-paper, and built a square cement base on the ground. I still regarded a light plant as a temporary arrangement until the power company came to its senses or another line could be negotiated—or some other miracle happened.

The Onan went in and was hooked up to the house wiring, which had been waiting for weeks, and by golly it worked. I went round the rooms turning the lights on and off as though I had not lived with electricity all my life. In the Vermont house it was an innovation as exciting to me as it must have been to New Yorkers half a century ago. This was my own personal, exclusive electric light. A thunder-storm which took out a transformer several miles away and left the village in darkness with its dinners cooling on its electric stoves never touched me. It was a further independence, like having my own water come out of my own rock. I had no water rates, and now no electric bills. The power was the same, one-hundred-and-ten-volt alternating current. I had fifteen hundred watts from the Onan, enough to run lights, toasters, radios, anything within reason. You pressed a light switch—take any switch, anywhere—there was a moment's breathless suspense while the message ran up the wire to the engine—and the light came on. We could *see*. You turned off the last light in the house—and the engine stopped. Wonderful.

Of course it ran on gasoline, which like kerosene was then rationed, but we got enough as we had no car to run as well. Because it was all so temporary, pending the miracle, the engine fed from a couple of five-gallon cans which stood beside it on the ground and had to be filled every week by deliveries from the village garage, along with its oil. *Nobody* could believe how much we ran it or how late at night, so more than once the engine died on us from lack of nourishment, and we had to finish out the evening with lamps. But after all we did have electric light.

We thought. The machine and the wiring and the installation had cost about seven hundred dollars, and the simplest kind of wartime lamps had come to nearly a hundred more. And worth every penny of it, we said every day. But before long the Onan began to show its age, or its temperament. It developed asthma, which affected the steadiness and power of the light it gave, and its automatic cut-off became erratic, so that it was likely to run all night unless I put on a coat over a dressing-gown and pyjamas and took a flashlight and went up through the dewy grass and pulled the switch, after the last light—always mine—was turned off. You could just hear it running if you listened, and you couldn't go to sleep without listening. By the time I had got back into bed I would be wide awake again, sometimes cold, always mad. I'd light a lamp, then, and read some more. Might as well be in Bermuda, with that set-up.

People came and tinkered it and coaxed it and shook their heads over it, and the implication began to emerge that I had been sold a pup. Nobody's fault, of course. I hadn't had it properly vetted by an Onan man before I bought it. There seemed not to be an Onan man nearer than Minnesota. By the end of that summer I had begun to move heaven and earth to get a brand new Kohler plant to go in next year. There was said to be a Kohler man only twenty miles away.

5.

*I*T WAS IN JULY OF THAT
eventful year 1945 that the bird Che-Wee made his unforeseen
entrance into our lives. Violent thunder storms and heavy
rains were the rule that season, and he was apparently blown
out of the nest a week or so too soon. He must have landed
with a bump in horrid wet grass and set out at once on his
own to find more comfortable surroundings. When I first saw
him he was making dubious progress across the front lawn under a pouring rain, and had travelled quite a way on half-
grown pinions and unsteady legs which allowed him to gain
about a foot of ground with each tremendous effort. There

wasn't another feathered creature in sight that day, and we never located the nest where he was born, but we used to see what we supposed was the rest of his family in the cherry hedge behind the house weeks later when they were full-grown.

We had no animals of our own, but there were half-wild farm cats which hunted all over the place, and probably only the weather had preserved him from their notice so far. I didn't want a baby bird, and I had no hope that such a drenched and exhausted specimen would live more than a few hours in any case. But at least I could save him from the cats, so I brought him in and dried him the best I could and got some bread soaked in warm milk down his throat and tucked him up in a Kleenex nest in a cracker box in front of the fire. When I went back to look at him an hour later, prepared to find only a little corpse, two bright eyes regarded me expectantly and his beak came open on a hoarse baby bird plea for More. I fed him again, and changed his Kleenex.

How Che-Wee made his unaggressive way into our unwilling hearts and became a cherished member of the family has been told elsewhere. He was a nuisance, and he still is, but we love him and he owns us. He has a little travelling-cage with a fitted flannel jacket which goes inside a zipper bag, and in this he migrates to New York each autumn and back to Vermont in the spring, with sometimes an extra trip or two during the winter. In the train when luncheon is served in the parlor car he has a snack through the bars—lettuce, fruit-juice or milk out of a teaspoon, whatever is going—and when he arrives at his destination he takes possession of his recovered belongings at either end with visible delight.

He prefers the country, I think, but finds New York very interesting. He's a very interested bird, anyway. Nothing bores him. He will listen enthralled to the dullest conversation or radio program. And he has his daily duties, all self-imposed —his supervision of my morning toilet and make-up from a well-chosen perch on a towel-rack or glass shelf in the bathroom, his own bath and the careful grooming of his feathers to follow, his attendance in the kitchen during the preparation of meals, his grim joy-rides on the typewriter-carriage while I work, and the frequent inspection of his dish-gardens where somebody plants birdseed which comes up green and must be kept mowed by him. If there is nothing else to do he can always put in a profitable half hour combing out his feathers again and tidying himself for possible visitors, or practicing his singing. Che-Wee is a lesson in the art of living. He can't even read—so far as I know—to entertain himself, but he is never idle or aimless or sorry for himself. Even his resting, bunched up cosily on one foot with the other cuddled into his breast feathers, is purposeful and happy.

At the end of the same summer I succeeded in getting the bathroom moved into the smallest bedroom upstairs, which required a dormer window added for head room over the tub, and I had the bathroom-that-was converted back into a bedroom with a lavatory in the big closet, in which they cut a window. With bamboo wallpaper and a Scotch plaid bedspread, this room inevitably became Will's territory.

More wallpaper went on during the summer. We had got to the upstairs now—yellow roses in Mother's bedroom, red ones in mine, pink ramblers in the attic study, fish in the new bathroom—until I was stopped cold by being unable to find anything to go with the peach-colored blankets which so enlivened the guest-room and which swore at any of the usual floral papers, and had to try again the following year, as it wasn't a light enough room to use blue or green tones on the walls. Every room looked bigger and gayer as the last traces of the former owners gave way to my own taste, and the worst of our makeshifts and inconveniences and economies began to be ironed out. The coal furnace was definitely too much for us, and so was the hot-water stove. Before I shut up the house that autumn I placed an order for an oil-burner. Nobody made any rash promises about when I would get it, but the war was over now. Or was it?

Meanwhile, each time that Will spent a week or two on the place delightful new discoveries outdoors had been made. He at once began a bird list, the brightest item of which was a pileated woodpecker which passed within a few feet of his head, to the intense surprise of both, on one of his first days there, and was not seen again till years later, up in the woods. The comparison of these northern hills with the New Jersey countryside of his boyhood produced mysterious notations and contemplative murmurs and sometimes downright excitement which I in my mere novel-writing ignorance could not always fully share.

George Swanson, artist on several of Will's expeditions and a great gardener by avocation, came for a spring visit, and the two of them once returned from a walk wearing Cheshire-cat smiles and cherishing a tired handkerchief which had been made into a bag to bring back to me a pink ladyslipper, complete with root, which was reverently planted in an appropriate spot under a butternut tree nearer the house, where it has bloomed sturdily ever since—except when the bud was nipped off by a passing woodchuck too impudent even to eat it. George had let out a yell accompanied by a rude shove to prevent Will from treading on it as he ambled characteristically through the woods with bird-glasses glued to his eyes. We all went back up the hill immediately to behold the glade where the ladyslippers grew—a small colony of them running down into a swamp where very pale blue violets bloomed with their roots in water.

I have yet to count and identify the violets on the place—all shades of blue and purple, yellow and veined white, all sizes from minute white specks right in the lawn, scrooging down under the blades of the lawn-mower, to the largest whites I have ever seen anywhere. Closed blue gentians grow trustfully in the middle of the old rocky road, impossible to cars, which runs up the hill to our back line and beyond. Bluets are my peculiar personal joy, as I had never seen them before I came to Vermont, and they respond so heartily to transplanting and bloom round the rock walls like floral popcorn balls, with no visible foliage and a delicate range of tint from pure white to lavender blue. Canada violets were new to me too, though most of the favorites of my mid-West childhood holidays—spring beauties, anemones, red trillium, dutchman's breeches, and dog-tooth violets—are here in our woods where nothing has ever been picked or pulled up by greedy motorists and campers.

One of the many things I promised myself that I would *not* have in this book was a lot of purple patches about views, and gardens, and the general heartbalm of life in the country. Everybody has already read that somewhere else. My experience is interesting only as it differs from that of people who went to the country either because it was a lifelong dream-come-true and existed beautifully thereafter, or because they had to make a living out of it and almost died laughing at their hardships. I came to the country as it were almost by accident, and I am still there more or less to my own astonishment. It sort of grew on me, that's all.

Still, it happened to me, and there are certain recognizable stages in my, shall we say, conversion. You need an extra set of eyes and ears for country living, or rather your senses tend to atrophy in town and it is like having new ones when you start to perceive things not connected with traffic, shops, and a social calender. Week-ends and holidays don't count for this. You have to belong.

I shall only mention, as briefly as possible, that by now we had learned to watch each day in the spring, almost each hour, while the wooded hillside opposite the house and the steep slope of Haystack Mountain to the north changed from dull grey patched with sharp evergreen to the fragile yellows and pinks and greens of opening tree buds. Later on, the unimaginable variations on the single color green as the first leaves come out are to me even more exciting than the more famous shift to bold autumn color in October. There are a few days in May when the fern fists on foot-high stalks at the edge of the woods below the house make a pattern and a new green all their own. Each old apple tree has its individual tints of leaf and bud before it blossoms. And quite suddenly one day the hay is high enough to ripple and shine under the breeze—and summer is here again.

It can get really hot during the day, even at this altitude, so that one hunts the breezy side of the house and shifts the tea-table and chairs into the shade there, and the clink of ice in tall, mint-sprigged glasses is a pleasant sound. We are fortunate in being able to picnic on the lawn on any of three sides, which permits a movable feast on the east, south, or west, according to the temperature and the direction of the wind.

To collapse in a chosen spot with things to sip and munch at the end of a hot afternoon and contemplate one's achievement with trowel, rake, or paint brush, is one of the most satisfying aspects of the life we live here. A big yellow *papilio* floats round and round the house from left to right on a sort of beat—we think it is always the same butterfly on his lawful occasions. Hummingbirds zoom past our heads on their way to the delphiniums in the perennial border, and perform their pendulum courtship dance above the lilac bush or the scarlet monarda. Since the natural rock pool on the south terrace was finished it is in perpetual use as a bird-bath, and the purple finches, goldfinches, white-throats, cat-birds, juncos, and chipping sparrows, to say nothing of the robins, have no objection to its technical owners drinking tea only a few feet away from their splashings.

No less an authority than Mr. Van de Water has set it down in print that annuals aren't worth the trouble in Vermont because of the short summer, but don't believe a word of it. The best one can do, there are always gaps in the perennials' blooming time when nothing much is happening, and we can't get along without our annual sowing of cosmos, nasturtiums, and phlox at the very least. Zinnias succumb to the first touch of frost, and some years it is true they have a very brief blooming. They are also out of favor with us now because they seem always to require insecticides and so cannot come into the house for fear of making Che-Wee sick when he eats the bouquets. But the annual phlox goes on and on after frost and is sometimes almost all there is left to cut for the vases.

To be able to pick enough wild strawberries or red raspberries or blackberries for lunch free gratis in just a few minutes without getting out of sight of the house is something I shall never come to take for granted. We have set out some fancy raspberry canes and strawberry plants from the catalogues, which bear bigger, darker, sweeter fruit—but I get more of a bang out of the ones God gave us. Our apple trees are very old, but the strawberry apple still bears generously, and though the fruit won't keep long it is very special and the breed is getting rare. Some people even try to tell us there is no such thing as a strawberry apple, but Starr Cooper says that is what we have, and it makes sauce like nothing you have ever tasted if cold-packed in glass jars and covered with warm syrup and processed three solid hours over a slow fire. During the third hour it turns coral pink, and it should be served ice cold with cookies.

Don't tell me that applesauce will process in twenty minutes, because I already know that. But it will be just applesauce.

6.

WHEN WE ARRIVED EARLY
in May 1946 the Onan had been overhauled and it was making light, but the new Kohler was already there in its crate at the garage. A few days later on a sharp windy morning of that backward spring it was driven up our road in the garage truck, followed by a grey Plymouth containing two other men, one of whom was introduced as not the same Kohler expert already mentioned to me, but something just as good which had just come out of the Navy. The garage had always

been the soul of courtesy, but cars were their job after all, and not light plants, and the implication was plainer than words: Here's your electrician, now please leave the rest of us in peace.

The contribution from the Navy, whose name was Elmer LaFlamme, had the straightest eye I ever encountered and he looked cold. There was a fire in the furnace but a hospitable impulse on my part to ask them all in for a cup of coffee in the kitchen was lost in the shuffle of unloading the heavy crate at the chicken-house, and we all stood shivering around the sulky Onan while Elmer made it tactfully clear to me that the chicken-house in its present condition was no place to install a beautiful new Kohler direct from the factory. It wanted a cement floor, weather-tight roof and walls, and proper ventilation.

The only answer seemed to be to rebuild the chicken-house on the same site. They said there was enough good timber in it, a weathered silver grey, to make a smaller and quite sound house. I was at a loss, however, for anyone to do the rebuilding job, as labor of any kind was very scarce, until Elmer said he had a brother who might take it on. I asked for an estimate from his brother and said we would go ahead. But the Kohler must come first, to be installed at once on its own pedestal alongside the Onan, which would act as a spare in case of a breakdown. The cement floor and the new house could be constructed around them, during the summer.

I was working now against time on the final typing of *The Light Heart*, and so took very little notice of what went on in the chicken-house while the Kohler was being inaugurated. The Onan was still giving trouble in spite of expert nursing by Elmer, the weather stayed cold, and the furnace was driving us crazy, without even a full-sized boy to shake it down and deal with the ashes each day. There still wasn't an oil-burner available from the local plumber, who had had our order for about seven months, and we had Che-Wee to worry about now. Birds are subject to chills, and if the fire went out some night and he caught cold I would have it on my soul. So we made a lot of extra trips up and down the cellar stairs, which were something of a death-trap even after Mother suddenly got heroic with a hammer and nailed up a handrail.

Late one night after I had turned out my light I thought again of Che-Wee, trustfully asleep in his cage in the alcove downstairs—the house had been chilly all evening and the wind howled outside. If I went down and opened the damper and let the fire burn up higher and read for another half hour before checking it again for the night. . . . Mother's door stood open and her light was out. If I just nipped down quietly in the dark without putting on the staircase light. . . . I felt for my slippers and reached for my dressing-gown. I knew the stairs so well now, even in the dark. . . . And then there was a ghastly crunching sound as my left foot doubled under me on the step and I landed not very heavily at the bottom.

A lot of lights went on after that, and I hobbled into the downstairs bedroom where Mother made up the bed while I sat still, trying not to be sick, and the ankle swelled like a balloon being blown up, till it was about as big as a basketball. Nothing in the way of hot or cold applications had any effect on its size or gathering color. I hadn't the nerve to call the village doctor after midnight on a Saturday, so with the aid of aspirin I endured it till a reasonable hour on Sunday morning. He took one look and wanted an X-ray, of course, and there proved to be a small bone broken in an awkward place, so that in no time at all I found myself on the sofa in my living-room with a plaster cast up to the knee. Will was in Venezuela again, where only the year before he had broken his own left ankle in some impromptu gymnastics with a sloth and a ladder.

Elmer was to finish up the Kohler job the next day, and when he came into the house to say that it was accomplished and test the lights and condole with me about the ankle, I asked him as a favor to shake down the furnace and scoop out the ashes, and just happened to mention my now desperate need of the oil-burner I couldn't get.

Within another week an oil-burner was completely installed and making heat, turning itself on and off by a thermostat in the dining-room with never a more than four-degree variation in temperature. My unfilled order had been amiably cancelled with a man who had plenty of places to put oil-burners if he ever got one, and Elmer, who was able to get one occasionally, had put in one of his. The new Kohler, which ran like a dream from the beginning and brought with it a thirty-five-gallon tank which was buried in the ground behind the chicken-house, made the thermostat quite dependable. (Because the burner had a low-voltage control Elmer had to adapt it to the Kohler by substituting a high-voltage thermostat, which turns on a forty-watt light bulb down cellar, which starts the Kohler, which then runs the oil-burner. To shut off the heat, the thermostat when satisfied turns off the light bulb. The bulb, being connected to the incoming power line to the oil-burner, turns off the burner. Simple, isn't it!)

With the Corona on a lap-board and my cast on a cushion I finished the printer's script of *The Light Heart* in a peace of mind and a controlled room temperature which was sheer bliss. And Che-Wee didn't get pneumonia.

7.

W<small>E</small> HAVE COME NOW
to the first turning point in my attitude towards the place.
With permanent, automatic heat and light, and civilized bathroom arrangements, the Vermont house ceased to be a sort of
glorified camping-out place and began to resemble a home. We
still lacked the last amenities, such as an automatic hot-water
system—some mysterious gadget was unobtainable even to
Elmer—and a refrigerator which made its own ice. The three-
burner oil stove was adequate only to the simplest cooking,
and had no oven. Any serious attempt to heat the house in
really bad weather would be a sinful waste of fuel without
the addition of double windows, repairs to the foundation, and
insulation in the attic.

Berlin had fallen a year ago, but there was still nothing you could call peace, and the things Russia was saying had a dreadful similarity to the things Germany had been saying ten years ago. Each time the radio and newspapers reminded me of this I reminded myself not be be a chump. I didn't have to remind myself of how when I was in England during the repeated summer crises of the mid-Thirties we would escape from London to somebody's country cottage for even a few hours with a sense of truant joy—nor of how tension and dismay lessened mile by mile as I travelled westward from London into Somerset during the anxious days of September, 1938—nor of how in the autumn of 1939 I watched my English friends transferring their most precious belongings, animal, vegetable, and mineral, from London flats to cottages in the country if they were lucky enough to have one—nor of how cheerfully when the need did arise the same people doubled up and took in other people who had no refuge. These were three a.m. thoughts that came without being invited. I did not—at least in broad daylight—expect another war. At least not soon. But—when it came, *if* it came, we who were now only middle-aged would all be too much older to be useful—and so. . . .

Well, first I looked into the matter of double windows to conserve fuel. That was only sense, no matter what happened, or if nothing happened at all. The old days of balancing on a ladder with a heavy storm-window catching the wind have gone. You can get windows divided into top and bottom sashes which hook on from inside, with screens to alternate in summer—and which theoretically a woman can handle alone. I counted up windows. I ordered fourteen, and little ones for the bathroom dormer, and Elmer put them on. Each one had to be tediously cut down with his little power saw which rode round on the wheelbarrow, or else added to with small strips, before it could fit the crazy angles of the frames on this old house. Each one had to be painted white, and then the metal catches had to be screwed on to both window and casing.

During the time this took, the deer began leaving little sharp hoof-marks each night in the garden where the peas and lettuce and beets were coming up—they go for beets—although for some reason they had not yet cleaned us right out. Fencing was hard to get and very expensive. It was becoming a habit now to consult Elmer, who seemed to know everything, and the upshot of that was that he took a day off from the windows and put in a charged wire which ran off a battery, around the whole yard and garden, open only on the side where the house and road were. That strange combination of curiosity and caution which is a deer quite literally sticks its neck out— it approaches a suspicious object like a clucking wire nose first, and gets badly stung where it hurts. The more experienced deer sense the eddy of current around the wire, or possibly recognize the steady *cluck-cluck* as a warning, and don't even try. It doesn't bother birds because when they sit on it they aren't grounded.

The ordinary charge of an electric fence is not very strong —that is, a man can touch it without yelling. But our fence is grounded on a two-inch pipe instead of the usual smaller one, just because there happened to be a piece handy, and it carries an awful wallop. More than once after its installation we noticed the deer standing in twos and threes at the edge of the woods with their heads together, gazing wistfully towards our succulent cabbages and beets, with the wicked wire running between, and we could imagine the conversation: Well, mark my words, it's a daisy, you won't try it more than once, I can tell you.

The garden was a great success.

Next, we went into the matter of insulation, and bags of rock wool soon arrived and were stacked up in the barn. Elmer said he would put it in before the weather got cold, or find someone to do it. The "modern" methods of blowing the insulation material into the walls by a machine through a hole in the outside is practical only for newly built houses. In these old farm houses the intramural space is interrupted by big timbers which may occur almost anywhere and which cut off pockets of space which are impossible to reach and fill with the blower. The insulation packs and sags until its position next to an empty pocket becames visible even from the outside. Elmer's intention was simply to lay loose rock wool, not bats, several inches deep on the floor of the attic above the bedrooms, or on top of the bedroom ceilings, if that is clearer, which made a remarkable difference in the upstairs temperature at once. Then during later repairs to the bathroom walls where the plaster had suffered during the introduction of the dormer and plumbing, and which was on the cold side of the house, he removed lath on the inside enough to insert and pack rock wool into the two outer walls from floor to ceiling, finished off with wallboard and fresh paper, and again we congratulated ourselves on a most perceptible difference in the way the room received and held the heat from its register. To insulate the whole west and north side of the house as we expect to do, it will be quite simple to remove enough clapboards from the outside to insert and pack the rock wool from there without disturbing the wallpaper. After the clapboard is off, you drop a plumb-bob down between the walls to make sure the space is clear, so that the insulation can drop and pack all the way to the bottom. If the plumb-bob hits a timber, you have to measure down to the stoppage, remove another clapboard below it, and fill from there. And the difference in the cost of this operation, compared to the estimate by any professional insulators, is considerable.

Elmer's brother had not materialized, being very busy elsewhere, but having promised us a plant-house built by a La-Flamme Elmer went to work on it himself, first taking down the old chicken-house—which practically came apart in his hands—and sorting out the good lumber in tidy stacks, throwing aside the rotten parts in a pile to give away as sugar wood or junk. Then, with the engine running under a tarpaulin, he put in a cement floor and built a small square tidy house with three windows, a sliding door, and a tar-papered roof, and room at one end for a tool-bench. When the tension of the cable which came up from the big house produced not even a creak, and when in its first winter the little house stood up under the worst snows since '88, he seemed mildly surprised and pleased. We had been lucky enough to catch him at a loose end after the Navy, before he re-opened his civilian electrical business, and tinkering this place happened to appeal to him as a form of holiday. When I apologized for the difference in the wages he asked here and what he could have been earning as an expert in his line, he remarked that after four years in the Navy, routine was something he could do without for a while. And routine was just what we hadn't got any of.

Reliable electricity made it possible to use a small automatic pasteurizer for the milk, and so do away with the primitive thermometer-in-a-kettle method we had used until now. We could not bring ourselves to use raw milk, and it is at last dawning on even the local die-hards that undulant fever is not a thing to fool around with. If you get it you've got it, and there is no immunity to future attacks and no permanent cure. Its many masquerades, such as rheumatic fever, which is often diagnosed by mistake, have caused its own particular menace

49

to be minimized too long, and while you can still buy both raw milk and pasteurized in bottles at the village store, the sales of the pasteurized are gaining. Contrary to obstinate belief by many people, it has been demonstrated that they cannot tell one from the other in a blindfold test if the pasteurizing has been properly done, nor does the cream suffer. Overheating does make it taste different, of course, and that frequently happened with the makeshift double-boiler method we had had to depend on. The little pasteurizing machine cost about $25 from the mail order house, and it turns itself off and turns on a buzzer when the milk is ready to be cooled. It is one of our favorite possessions.

The three-burner open-faced kerosene stove was now dispensed with, when Elmer put a small oil-burner into the range in place of the old wood-burning fire-box. This began as a Lynn burner with a hand-filled three-gallon tank, which was used up about every twenty-four hours. It later acquired a constant-level valve and fed direct from a two-hundred-and-seventy-five gallon tank in the woodshed. The burner is never turned entirely out, so the stove and the kettle on it are always warm, and when the screw is turned up a good hot fire, including the oven, is soon available. No wood, no coal, no fuss, no dirt.

By now it was haying time again, and a different arrangement had to be made as the man who had taken it before no longer required extra hay. It was done most efficiently this year, with a swarm of machinery, even to a baler, and there were no flies.

I don't know which of us mentioned the sugar-bush first, but Elmer and I agreed that it was a pity to have let it go to waste all these years. One day he borrowed the key to the sugar-house and spent a while surveying the equipment. His report was much less gloomy than any other opinion I had

had and I began to take notice. Always at the back of my mind had been the wish to see syrup made on the place, just as a lark. But now that the house could be used the year round, the sugaring might even be taken seriously. I began to explain that I had no idea how to go about getting someone to take charge of it, and realized that I was talking to a thoughtful silence.

Gradually I learned that he had taken over his father's sugar-bush at the age of fourteen and had run it at a profit thereafter. He was farm born and bred, and often got homesick for the things that stood for. And much more acutely than I did then, he felt that a great mistake was being made to allow these old, established, productive New England farms to become mere "summer places"—idle and wasted and empty at least nine months in the year, a total loss to a world which needs every ounce of produce that can be got from its soil. His father was getting old, and had retired into a comfortable house in town, but he had never lost interest in the things he had always loved to do. . . . When I broke in with excited questions, Elmer couldn't promise anything—yet. But it might be that his father would like to give us the benefit of his experience, as a sort of hobby, and there was no better timber and sugar man in Vermont. . . .

We neither of us rushed into the thing. I was afraid of the financial outlay, and he was afraid, I think, of being tied down in case he wanted to do something else. While the pros and cons went on in our minds and conversation, the summer ripened to autumn before our eyes, and the place sat there waiting in the sun, its hayfields green again with the rowan, its apple trees turning red with fruit, its maple leaves brightening towards the frost—acquiescent, hopeful, so patient and so good, but unable to do its job without our help.

We got as far as pencilled figures on little scraps of paper

—a new evaporator pan, luckily the front one, sixty dollars—a big power-saw to cut the wood for the fires, fifty dollars—paint for the buckets and tanks—bricks and cement to repair the arch in the sugar house—a new smoke-stack—more labor (always the biggest item) to get in wood before the sap began to run, and a helper after; two helpers, unless his father would come and boil—a dreigh and a sled for the gathering tub and a tractor to draw it, all second-hand, and I could trust him to get a good bargain on any sort of machinery. But it all added up to money.

Of course I had meant to spend frivolously whatever extra money I might have, now that the war was over. I had promised myself a lot of new clothes, more than I really needed, while I was still young enough to enjoy them, and more books—expensive ones—and I wanted to get back to England soon. . . .

But if I let Elmer go now I might never have another chance to get the work done by a man I had so much confidence in. Next year might be too late, he would be established somewhere else. If I made a deal with him now and the sugaring was a success, and we decided to go on with it the following year, and the year after that, then he might take on the hay too, and I wouldn't have to have strangers in to cut it. Even if we didn't manage to pay for the equipment out of the earnings, even if we didn't break even for years to come, wasn't it worth *doing*. . . . It seemed as though an investment in productiveness, in a harvest which could be seen and tasted in a hungry world, and even sold to pay for more equipment to increase the yield, made more sense than buying paper bonds or burying dollars in a crock under the hearth. The squirrel in me roused again. Each spring the sap ran, and nobody took it and made it into syrup and stored it away. . . .

It would want all the extra money I had, and more. There could be no compromise with the venture once it was begun. Either I must do without perhaps unimportant but desirable things I had begun to see my way to, and put the money here, or I could enjoy myself in other directions and leave things here exactly as they were, without further ambition or fruition. Will had helped me to buy the place, and as it stood now it more than fulfilled our first intentions. What I spent on it beyond that and what I went without was up to me to decide.

This was the second turning point. Slowly, quietly, without any blinding revelations or trumpet fanfares, but as it were inevitably, from within, the land I had acquired so lightly had begun to own me. The day came before long when I said to Elmer, "I'll take it on if you will." And we shook hands.

8.

WHEN I LEFT FOR NEW
York that year a second new Kohler, twin to the other,
had replaced the unreliable Onan as auxiliary, with an ingeni-
ous hook-up which practically guaranteed us against loss of
electric power. Normally they share the load, the elder taking the furnace and the pressure pump, Junior carrying the
lights and appliances. This way neither of them runs continu-
ously enough to deteriorate, and between them I have 3000
watts, with ample allowance for overload. But there is a little
switchboard, and if either engine gives trouble or needs a
rest, the whole load can be transferred to the other until the
arrival of a repair man. Which at present simply means, until
Elmer can deal with it.

But our plants don't break down. Every now and then one

of them is given a vacation to be overhauled, but they are faithful beyond all expectation, partly because of careful tending, partly because it is their Kohler nature. Elmer says that in the Navy, where they are used for power on the smaller boats, he has seen them running practically under water, and a job like ours is pie for them.

I am not such an idiot about machinery as Will is, but I'm no genius, and Elmer thought he could make it simple enough so that I could do the switch-over to one engine myself from the double hook-up, and I was willing to try. It was impressed on my mind that in no circumstances must they *ever* both be switched on to the same circuit at the same time, and I was shown how to accomplish the transfer without bringing about this disaster. When, with both engines disconnected, I first attempted to put these instructions into practice and went through the motions at the switchboard, Elmer silently covered his face with both hands and shuddered.

It took him a lot more thought and another hour or two of readjustments before he got things fixed so that I could never do it that way again. Now, by the removal of a fuse first, I am safe. The engines look very sweet, sitting side by side, father and son, just alike, in their battleship grey paint, and I wouldn't part with them if the power company came in on its knees, which is very unlikely. Junior cost more because the price had jumped again before I got him, and he has an extra gimmick or two. All they ask of me is enough gasoline—we buried a five-hundred-gallon tank behind the plant house when Junior came—and the weekly administration of oil, which even Will could do without getting into trouble. I love them like a mother.

The next addition to our family was the John Deere tractor, rather battered and very second-hand, but sound in wind and willing as all get-out. Nothing on the place works so hard and gives so little trouble as Old John. His rear tires are bigger around than I am, and he owns a pair of spare wheels with ice-grippers on them. He is so simple to drive that I have learned to do it myself, and so noisy you can't hear yourself speak. He will haul anything that has a place to put a draw-pin or hook a chain, and run anything that has a belt. Almost he smiles. We have got very attached to him.

I first met him when I went up for a few days at the end of January and found deep snow. He was breaking out the sugar-roads then—nosing his stubborn way along in a depth that nearly covered his front wheels, often getting stuck, always getting out again. And the tracks he made were beautiful. Each time it snows you iron out your roads again and keep the ruts firm. This saves time and trouble later on when you are ready to take your gathering tub through on the dreigh.

After I returned to New York they had a snowfall that beat anything in years, and it was too much for Old John's front wheels. Elmer had to hire a caterpillar tractor to open up the roads again. Crawlers will go anywhere and do anything, and will stand almost on end without falling over backwards on you.

When I arrived back just as sugaring time began, Old John was hauling the dreigh, which is a Thing consisting of two poles bolted to a bolster that rides on a sled to which it is attached by a king-pin. The front ends of the poles rest on the heavy sled runners, and the back ends drag along the ruts, like the Indian *travois* which hitched on behind their horses to transport household goods and occasionally squaws and papooses. This primitive contraption can go where wagons can't, and it won't tip over. Something of a similar nature was doubtless in use before wagons were dreamed up, and I am reminded of the *Punch* cartoon by the man who signs himself merely Geo. M. and always does the historical-times jokes. This one is captioned: *The Inventor of the Round Wheel Gives a Demonstration.* It depicts a small, browbeaten, skin-clad Neolithic man pushing an ancestor of the wheelbarrow, made of a rather nicked and lopsided solid stone wheel attached by thongs to an axle with two long handles. His skin-clad audience of neighbors is in painful stitches of derisive laughter.

The Vermont dreigh is used to bring in uncut logs, to carry stacks of sap buckets, or the gathering tub, or any awkward thing. They loaded it with columns of buckets set one inside the other, and I rode on the high front crossbar close behind the tractor—making sure my feet didn't get pinched off at the turns—and watched them scatter buckets. Before the sap begins to run the buckets are left beneath each tree, and when you go round to tap you have only to carry the spouts and the covers.

I like to see anything done which is done superbly well, from ballet to boxing. Elmer and his helper, Art, had scattered buckets since they were children, and there wasn't a waste motion, and what they did had a rhythm and economy of effort that formed a definite pattern to a spectator who sat still behind the tractor and looked on. The capacity of a tree to yield sap is gauged not by the size of its trunk but by the spread of its branches. Therefore a man scattering buckets always looks up as he approaches a tree, and drops one, two, or three as the tree warrants.

The men in their bulky mackinaws and thick trousers tucked into boots would leave the dreigh, each carrying a heavy tower of buckets as tall again as he was, gripped under his right arm. Theirs were the first tracks—unless you count racoons and bobcats—to be made in glistening snow often three feet deep over uneven ground. As they reached each tree their chins came up to see the top, and the buckets were nudged off the bottom of the tower, which grew shorter at each pause. They seldom looked behind them, where the buckets landed. And though it was bad going, and they dropped into holes and staggered while the bucket towers swayed above them, and their progress was very casual, it had somehow almost the makings of a ballet—the long, effortless stride which sank knee-deep or more at every step—the zig-zag route between the trees—the pause, the upward tilt of the chin, the fall of the bucket, and on—patient, unhurried, me-thodical, good-tempered, as all good work on the land must be.

The tapping is done with a brace-and-bit, and a good deal of care, not too deep into the tree and just above the snow-line. The snow may melt while it hangs there, and the joke goes that if you put it too high you will need a ladder to reach it when the thaw comes. You pick a spot on the tree where the bucket can hang rigid against the trunk, sometimes chipping away a knob of bark to make the bucket sit firmly. The south side of the tree flows best. The bit goes in at the slightest up-ward angle, and even before the spout is hammered in, the clear, cold sap is dribbling down the trunk. For efficiency, it takes a man to bore, a man to drive in the spout and hang the bucket from it, and a boy to hang the covers.

If more than one bucket to a tree is hung, they must be staired, one slightly above the other. No one seems to know why, but Elmer and Art knew that if they didn't do it that way they would catch heck from the Old Man, who had him-self rebuilt and painted the arch, so *that* was done right, and had consented to boil for us. Whatever your outlay or your equipment or your sap yield, your profit and your syrup reputation are in the hands of the man who boils. We had the best.

There had not been time after we made up our minds to undertake this thing to bring down enough wood, and we had to buy some extra slabs, which hurt us as the hillside was full of stuff crying to be used, and we had given away the leftovers from the old chicken-house. There had not even been time to re-paint all the buckets and the tanks, and so we were much plagued by leakage that first year. But the first time you put your lips to a brimming bucket of ice-cold sap while it still hangs on the tree is an experience you won't forget, especially if it is your own tree. The sap is clear as water in the white-painted bucket, and not really sweet, if your palate is prepared for syrup—it has a distinctly woody aftertaste.

Thirty-five to fifty gallons of sap boil down to one gallon of syrup in the flat, partitioned evaporator pans in the sugarhouse, and the white steam which hangs like a fog over the interior and pours out the open flaps at the top does smell like all the syrup in the world, the essence of sweetness. The weight of the finished syrup is ordained by law—eleven pounds to the gallon in the can. And it must appear on the printed label which is also required if you are going to take your syrup to the market.

The dreigh with the gathering-tub—which is called the tommyhawk, don't ask me why—makes the rounds every day when the sap is really running, if you get a good season with warm sunny days and cold nights. We are lucky in having a double bush—that is, the lower end of it near the house runs early in the season and in the morning sun, and the trees up on the hill are later to start and fill their buckets for afternoon gathering. There is also a tradition that the mixture of sap from trees on both high and low land improves the flavor.

The 1947 season was for us only a sighting shot. We made some good syrup, proved that our equipment would function, and found out what we still lacked. Paint, first of all—it is heartbreaking to see a bucket leaking like a sieve on to the snow as it hangs on the tree; some additional new buckets, metal by choice, to replace the worst of the wooden ones and to make use of more young trees which were ready to be tapped; wood to burn, and a lean-to at the sugar-house to stack it in—all the makings for that except the aluminum roof could be found on the place. Next year, we would be all set in time. Next year we could really make some syrup. And the year after that, fifteen hundred buckets, just as they said.

9.

*I*T IS VERY GOOD FOR
one to come full-fledged upon vast tracts of ignorance in one's
cosmos. When I bought the house in Vermont I thought I
had been around. I had crossed the Atlantic twenty-four
times, with about as many voyages to Bermuda in between. I
had been to California often enough to lose count. I knew the
Tidewater country, the tip of Florida, and the Maine coast.
Even Haiti. (Once was enough for that.) I had written thir-
teen books and two plays, and was pretty much at home in
the cock-eyed world of the theater and the even madder ter-
rain of the moving-picture studios both here and in England.

To say nothing of a few scientific expeditions, which are somewhat balmy too.

Then I took up farming.

It *looked* fairly simple. I was familiar with its environs by the time I began, I knew people who apparently could do it on their heads, I thought we all spoke the same language. But when we got down to business on making this place produce, Elmer and his father, Starr Cooper and even Art, must often have wondered if I was half-witted, and I certainly felt sometimes that they must be deliberately obfuscating the issue. They on the other hand were discussing matters which were to them so obvious as hardly to need words and I must have appeared to them to be wilfully dense. Finally I would get a glimmer that we were coming at the same thing from opposite directions with no bridge in the middle, and ask some question which revealed the extent of my blankness, to which they would reply in words of one syllable, and there would be a relieved round of "*Oh*, I thought you meant—" and "*No*, I thought you knew—" and another crisis was safely past. Their patience and good manners and my willingness to learn saw us through. But I am not by nature meek, and they have had a lot to bear.

There was the matter of the caterpillar tractor. When the snowfall got too much for Old John during that first year's sugaring, and Elmer had to bring in the caterpillar to help him, I failed to see the significance. There was some talk about caterpillars after I went back that spring, and the hireling (which had not yet been reclaimed by its owner) went through its tricks for me, with its winch and so on, and I knew that Elmer regarded caterpillars highly and even hankered for one on the place. But as he is in love with anything which has wheels that go round, from watches to diesel locomotives, I made allowance for that. When I once asked the price of caterpillars second-hand and he told me, I whistled and said lightly, "It's too much!" A long time went by before what are affectionately called crawlers came up again. When they did, I realized to my astonishment that he was under the impression that he had put in a formal request for one and been categorically refused. So then we had to start all over again.

In June we bought T-20.

He cost two thousand dollars, second-hand. He's a rather miniature crawler, with only ten-inch treads, and he was once bright red, but he has a rugged career of logging jobs behind him. Even Old John was a bit stove in when he came to us, with a crumpled right rear fender—I bent the other one to match, the first time I backed him into the barn. T-20 had rubbed himself bare of paint on all projecting points of his anatomy, trees seemed to have fallen across his hood, his vestigial fenders were accordion-pleated, and his driver's seat had to be tied together with string. But his engine is stout and willing, and his strength is as the strength of ten. (Because his heart is pure. Tennyson.)

Whereas Old John croons songs to himself on the hills, and is frankly pigeon-toed, and has a certain *je m'en fich'isme* when he can't quite make it, T-20 is flat-footed and four-square and earnest, never gives in, and grunts and scowls at his work. If he can't pull it he can push it, like an elephant piling teak, and if he can't go forward he can put still more power into backing. He turns on a dime and *g-r-r-r* goes at it again. When T-20 takes hold, whatever it is has got to come. Even Old John comes out of mudholes like a cork out of a bottle. T-20 is all business, and there isn't a spare inch on him to give a lady a ride, though Old John has broad accommodating fenders either side of the driver. He could not by any means supercede Old John. He couldn't run the saw, and hauling a mower or wagon during haying isn't in his line. But for snow work and lumber work T-20 is the thing.

All summer long except in haying time we took the fine days to do our logging—wood for the sugar-house fires next year, wood for the fireplace in the house, wood which must be moved from where it had lain for years across the unused sugar-roads, dead standing trees which would carry forest fire like torches to the branches of healthy trees near by. It was a singular satisfaction to me, whose exercise has always consisted mainly of running a typewriter, with the additional handicap of a recent illness, to find that by taking it easy and watching how it was done and not hurrying I could myself hook the heavy chains around a log the same as Art did—it takes little strength, only knack—and see them hold as well as his did all the way along the road, skidding down behind T-20 to the open space above the brook where they were to be cut up.

In the old days men like Elmer's father would have been ashamed of anybody who couldn't go into the woods—without a tractor—and cut their two and a half cords a day, and pile it—at seventy-five cents a cord! Two men could do four to five cords a day, piled. And then they would walk sixteen miles at the end of the week to take their pay home to their wives, or to blow it on a handsome spree, and be back on the job again on Monday morning. A good many of them had French names and little formal education, and their sons were taught to use their hands and were sent to school as well, and it was a heritage worth having.

Everytime I see an ad in the paper announcing a new shipment of "genuine sugar-maple furniture" I wonder with a qualm if the lumber from which it was made came down from the wilds of Canada where the trees would never have been tapped anyway, or if another Vermont sugar bush had been sacrificed to a greedy impulse for ready cash. A sugar orchard which will bring $3500 spot cash will yield its owner up to $1000 yearly in syrup. Therefore a man who sells his maples to be cut down is believed to need his head examined, as it would take him only three or four years to get that money out in syrup and he would still have the trees. There can no longer be any alibi either about needing the money for a sick baby or whatever, because through the Farm Bureau's efforts any bank will lend him the money he would receive for the sale and few questions asked, just to enable him to keep the bush in production and save it from the ax. Some forty years ago maple trees bigger than most of those still standing on our land were cut away for logs—their stumps are still visible among the younger growth where our buckets hang each year. And if they had been left we could now set over two thousand buckets, many of them on three- and four-bucket trees.

T-20 had no winch when he came, and until we could get one for him and attach it to his behind, the dreigh was no good for the big stuff we had to get out because of damage, as it couldn't be loaded. So the big logs were dragged in a three or four log hook-up, and helped to re-make the road as they went. At first I winced to see the fern and baby evergreens in the center of the road-bed torn away by the dragging logs. But when the men gathered up the débris and cut back the small broken stuff at the sides for a few yards to show me how it would look when they had finished, and I saw how the growth sprang back and renewed itself and the gashes in the bark healed over in a matter of days, I became enthusiastic over unforeseen advantages.

Until we started to re-make the lost sugar-roads, often completely vanished to the untrained eye, treading out new tracks with T-20, cutting away the small saplings as he went, I had no idea of the variety and beauty of the land I owned. Even on rambles with Will, whose sense of direction is reliable where mine is non-existent, we had kept more or less to the main track. T-20, dragging his dreigh behind him to collect the small wood as it was cut from his path, branched out in all directions. It was rough going, where only teams had ever been before and that long ago, but nobody minded. With Elmer in the driver's seat, T-20 nosed out the invisible roads, scraping between new growth, halting while the saplings were axed down to let him pass, sometimes hung up on a stone in the middle of the track which had caught his rear axle, growling and clawing his way free again, shouldering through thick evergreen branches which had met across the road and which tried their best to brush me off the dreigh—fording unexpected brooks (we found two more) and scrabbling up steep banks—leaving his neat serrated prints in leaf-mould which had been undisturbed for years—T-20 opened up for me whole new acres of land.

There were groves of every size and variety of Christmas trees so dense that the ground beneath them was carpeted brown with needles. There were young beeches so close together that the sun made only yellow stripes between their slender trunks, and a patch of larger beeches more than ready to cut. Unlike the maples, beeches go bad from within when they reach a certain age, and unless cut for timber at their prime are good only for firewood, and gradually as they weaken become only a menace and a nuisance to be cleared away. There was a place of vast grey rocks, sheer as a ship's prow on three sides, with lovely vistas from their mossy summits. For the first time I saw where my boundary ran, all the way round, as Elmer had traced it out the previous winter. Meanwhile, myself being only a passenger, his woodsman's eye was marking what to come back for, and what to preserve. And now when the roads were only a little trimmed and made plain enough for even me to follow, I could find all these places again with the most tenderfoot guest, without having to rely on somebody else's sense of direction or attempting a compass. We could take up a picnic basket. . . .

Except for the bears, that is.

If they had told us when we bought the place that bears went with it we would probably have been incredulous to the point of rudeness. After all, New York City is only two hundred miles away. Foxes near the brook, deer in the garden, porcupines on the lawn, woodchucks under the porch, chipmunks in the attic—yes. But we were *not* prepared for bears in the road.

It was broad daylight in July, a hot sunny noon time, when I asked Elmer to drive me down to the mail-box to bring up some large parcels expected from Sears Roebuck. The road runs down hill between two hayfields and through a patch of deep woods where a brook flows under a culvert. The mail-box stands on the town road which is unpaved and thickly wooded on both sides. We drove down, waited at the fork for the mail-car, passed the time of day with the postman, who then drove on, turned our own car, and started back towards the house. Just above the brook Something crashed out of the woods on our right—the direction that the mail-car had taken—and crossed the road diagonally in front of us, going lickety-split for the woods on the other side. It was in full view for some seconds, during which there was dead silence in the car and I'm sure my jaw dropped. Then Elmer said in a rather shaken voice, "It's a *b-bear!*" and I knew I had seen what I saw.

We arrived back at the house more or less in a state of stupefaction, for it was a full-grown adult black bear, which would have weighed close to three hundred pounds, crossing the road within sight of the house on one side and the mail-box on the other. While Elmer is used to bears in their place, he was perhaps even more surprised to see one just there than I had sense enough to be. The mail-car had flushed it out of the woods on the right, and to its disgust it had met our car on the way home. There remained for me an indelible impression of the way its long hairy pants waved in the wind of its going. Will and I had seen what he thought were bear dens up our hill—that was not surprising or unlikely. But a bear had no business to be out in the open like this, unless it was up to something special, and the blackberries weren't ripe yet.

Since then it has been seen several times in the vicinity of our mail-box by other people, and we saw it ourselves on the hill not more than a hundred yards behind the house later in the year—we were walking into the field, and it also saw us and ducked back into the woods above the sugar-house. And during the autumn more than once we heard it calling from up there as the mating season came on.

That's a little near for comfort. Bears are not *supposed* to attack people unless their cubs are small and in attendance, but actually they are fairly aggressive all summer when full-grown, and one recently treed a friend of Elmer's who never even got a glimpse of any cub and was not inclined to argue the matter either, with the bear. The cubs trail the mother until well into the summer and she is likely to be cranky about it.

So what it amounts to is that we have been advised by unexcitable men who are hunters and woodsmen not to go up our side roads near twilight or early in the morning in cub season alone, unless prepared to shoot or to climb a tree with some alacrity. The bears, it seems, are gaining on us, and becoming a bit of a nuisance. It's a nice cheery thought, that the original New England wilderness is not irreparably tamed.

10.

Although che-wee
never took any notice of the birds he must have seen feeding
on the lawn and rocks outside the windows, nor seemed to
have any desire to explore the wide world beyond the pane of
glass which sheltered him from the weather, we still wondered
if sunlight and open air wouldn't be good for him. We knew
very well that it is often a mistake to "free" a bird you have
reared indoors, especially in a northern climate, as it has had

no experience of finding food and shelter, and has not been taught about owls and cats by its parents, and even if accepted by the flock instead of being killed by them as an outsider, it has not the wing strength to keep up with the migration. A house-raised bird stands a very slim chance on its own, barring a few unusual cases where a husky robin or crow has found its way back to its benefactors the following year after a successful migration. And except for a little while early in the spring when he has a morning fit of restlessness which makes him fly to and fro around the house as though he felt there was something he ought to be doing and wasn't—he is normal again before noon—nobody ever cared less about returning to Nature than Che-Wee. He likes his comforts and knows where the warmest corners are and where his favorite groceries are kept.

But a sunny summer day nevertheless always roused in us a feeling that maybe he ought to be out in it. One Sunday Mother and I between us with considerable labor tacked up window screen all the way round the small stone-flagged, covered stoop outside the back door of the kitchen, and sewed the joins together with strong black thread. All we wanted was something that would stay up for the rest of the summer and keep Che-Wee from getting lost in the yard. Like planting the garden each year, it nearly killed us, but we persevered, and finally the screen was really up, fastened to the posts and bird-proof.

Then we took off the screen door of the kitchen, so that if the house door was open you could walk straight out on to the stoop, which was just above ground level and looked on to the west lawn beneath a big butternut tree, with a stone wall and some large rocks near by. The space enclosed was big enough for a narrow table and four yachting chairs, and made a nice place for a tray luncheon or tea. We fastened some fresh apple and lilac branches to the posts, planted a small evergreen in a tub in one corner, and set a tall vase of field flowers on the floor—and it was quite a bower.

It was also the only thing that Che-Wee had ever been afraid of.

I took him on my finger to show him his new domain, and when we came to the threshold where the screen door had always been, he flew back into the kitchen with an alarmed yeep. I went after him and got him as far as the doorway again, with the same result. Finally when the door had stood open for some time he consented to ride out on my shoulder, but there was an apprehensive clutch to his claws and he was flat-headed and wary, and when I coaxed him to step from my finger on to one of the branches he clung there motionless and pop-eyed. The world, even seen from under the roof of the stoop, was much too big for him.

Gradually, by eating out there ourselves on trays, and keeping a dish of his seed on the table, we got him to enjoy it a little too, but he wouldn't stay there alone. If we went inside he came too, and he wouldn't go back without being carried. When we sat outside and offered him all the things he likes best to eat, we could get him to follow under his own steam—but he was still too cautious to fly through the doorway. He would go down on the kitchen floor and hop over the threshold and down on to the flagging, a step at a time. It was not until the very end of the summer that he ever ventured alone on foot across the threshold and then a short flight up to the table or a branch fastened to the post. Some dim little instinct several times made him want to go to sleep on the porch branch at twilight instead of his usual place above the kitchen sink. But the mountain nights are sometimes bitter cold, and he was used to a thermostated temperature now, so I always collected him before we closed up for the night. There was a feeding station on the butternut tree constantly used by his own family, as well as by nuthatches, indigo buntings, juncos, woodpeckers, cat-birds, and several kinds of sparrows, and we also put seed on the flat surface of a big rock close to the stoop. The wire screen between us and the birds seemed to reassure them—they could see us, and they would not let us get as near as that from the outside. But they seemed to know we could not reach them through the screen, and often a dozen assorted birds would feed there while we ate lunch or tea within six feet of them.

Che-Wee's attitude towards them was one of uninterested tolerance. He saw them, but he had his own seeds and perching places inside, and no apparent wish to share them or join the others. They were aware of him too and once out of curiosity a chipping sparrow flew against the wire and clung there peering in at him on his branch a few inches away. Che-Wee uttered a hoarse little scream of rage and stood his ground, flattened and menacing, with open beak. The inquisitive sparrow dropped off in surprise, and Che-Wee's crest came up—that's tellin' 'em.

The only other time he seemed to focus on the birds outside was one peaceful afternoon when about six or eight were feeding on the rock and Che-Wee was sunning himself on his branch in the corner while I sat reading in one of the chairs. All of a sudden he let out a series of loud, piercing yips which sounded like swearing and which caused all the birds on the rock to take off in a startled flurry of wings. Che-Wee sat still, with his crest up. Pretty soon all the other birds were back again as before and he took no further notice of them. What he had said in the way of atavistic bird-obscenities I can't imagine, but successful as it was in its effect he has never done it again.

His food preferences changed noticeably during his third summer. More and more he wanted sunflower seeds instead of canary seeds, so what was once just a treat or a reward became his main diet and he thrived on it. He still liked the canary song-food mixture, and picked out the black seeds I think are thistle. And he discovered ice cream—especially pink ice cream. He is not a greedy bird, and his manners are good. He will wait patiently on your shoulder for a spoon to come up with a tidbit on the tip of it. He will even stand a-tip-toe on the edge of the table beside your plate until his own share of salad or fruit or cereal is dished up to him in a glass ashtray, without rushing in to help himself from the big portion. But pink ice cream is too much for him. If bits from the tip of a spoon aren't offered often enough he will light on the edge of the dish and sink his beak into the mound. Its coldness always surprises him and he sits a moment fluffed out and thoughtful when it has gone down. He is not allowed to gorge, and one big bite is all he gets like that, but I am afraid he would eat pink ice cream until he died of it, if he got the chance.

In place of worms, which he wouldn't touch, he accepted a little scraped raw beef, all the better if it was still frozen. And he likes to drum with his feet on the big salt-shaker lid and lick what particles he can from around the opening. Milk is always good, best if it comes from the bowl of cereal which has had sugar on it. No one will believe that he knows the difference between shredded wheat and all other cereals even before he tastes it, and turns the others down, but he does, so help me. Any kind of fruit juice or jam is lovely stuff, but the latter is very hard to come by when one's diet is so carefully watched.

The little weed called shepherd's purse and the young plumes of blue grass from the edge of the lawn are his favorite green food, but any flowers which have a tube to hold honey, like nasturtiums or phlox are fun. And sorrel pods. And the rootstrings of spring onions with the dirt still sticking to them. And radish tails. A split pod full of young peas is a treasure to be cherished and returned to for hours. Just a trowelful of grassy sod and roots dumped on a newspaper makes a fascinating playground, and so do fresh branches of apple trees or young maple leaves. When he is left alone inside while we garden or make a trip to town for shopping, he always has a fresh supply of this kind of thing to occupy the time while we are gone, and a present of something different when we return.

Having become over a period of years accustomed to lavish tropical wild life, Will was inclined to complain that there weren't *enough* birds around the grounds of the place, so we put up more bird-houses and feeding-stations, and our neighborhood becomes increasingly popular each year. Purple finches now arrive in families and tribes, and I have seen a male purple finch and a male goldfinch drinking side by side in full sunlight at the edge of the pool. Even the timid indigo bunting appears more frequently as time goes on, and there are all kinds of sparrows except the undesirable English one.

Chipmunks thieved the seed faster than we could put it out on the rocks, which I wouldn't mind so much if they would eat it as the birds do, but they fill their cheeks and carry it away to hoard. When repairs were being made to the foundation at the back of the house a whole cache of seeds appeared from between the walls. So we devised feeders made of pie-tins nailed through the middle to the top of four-foot poles driven into the ground, and others to hang from the lower branches of trees. The smartest chipmunks still run up the trees and out along the branches to the feeders, but at least it's a little more trouble for them.

We buy a wild-bird mixture which has sunflower seeds in it for the finches and an assortment of smaller seeds for the sparrows, catbirds, and so on. The finches outnumber all the others, and nuthatches also like sunflower seeds—they wedge them into the bark and then hammer with their beaks to crack the shell, as their beaks are not strong enough to pinch it open as Che-Wee can. We therefore add half as much again of plain sunflower seed to each pound of mixed food as we distribute it. Both kinds come in twenty-five pound bags and because of mice and chipmunks are stored in large new garbage cans in the woodshed. After each heavy rain the feeders have to be taken down and scraped out and dried, or the leavings turn sour. A week's rainy weather can keep one fairly busy, or there will be a ring of fastidious, disappointed birds eyeing soggy food in a wet world. Since the news has spread that there is always a free lunch at Beebes' we live in an unceasing sound of wings, and the *teet-a-teet-teet* bickering of the finches as they eat is always audible through our open doors and windows.

I had heard only vaguely until now of peck-dominance—one of those delightful Anglo-Saxon semi-self-explanatory terms in which science rejoices and which it takes for granted, like the descriptive names of some species. (Yellow-bellied Sapsucker always sounds like an imaginative schoolboy epithet —"Ah gwan, you yellow-bellied sapsucker, you!"—and the Least Flycatcher—*E. minimus*—is logically the smallest of a dozen species, and the noisiest. When turning through a new bird-book I came across the Greater Yellowlegs, and inquired brightly if there was also a Least Yellowlegs. The ornithologists were ready for me, too. There is a Lesser one. Pursuing the subject, I learned that there is even a Bastard Yellowlegs, which added to my layman's joy in scientific nomenclature, and the Bristle-thighed Curlew must be something pretty special, to say nothing of something called the Grey Screaming Piha. Furthermore, the Solitary Sandpiper is sometimes found in flocks, and don't ever tell me what the Black-tailed Godwit looks like because I'd rather guess—while what caused the Flammulated Screech Owl and the Prothonotary Warbler to be so called will, I hope, remain blissful ignorance for me.) But the question of peck-dominance, or who is boss at a bird feeding station, is settled daily all over the place and always comes out the same.

It is Che-Wee's habit to perch on the lampshade near by when Will makes up his notes at the big table in the living-room, and if he was reading upside down when the well-known naturalist's observations were last totted up, this is what he learned:

"From July 22 to 30th a few notes were made on peck-dominance or tyrannization among several species and varying ages. The species observed were the following, in order of rarity to abundance:
(Total length in inches, and scientific names are included.)
Indigo Bunting (5.6) *Passerina cyanea*
White-crowned Sparrow (6.9) *Zonotrichia l. leucophrys*
Chipping Sparrow (5.37) *Spizella p. passerina*
Song Sparrow (6.3) *Melospiza m. melodia*
Junco (6.27) *Junco h. hyemalis*
White-throated Sparrow (6.7) *Zonotrichia albicollis*
Purple Finch (6.22) *Carpodacus p. purpureus*

77

The general order of dominance, checked and rechecked, day after day was as follows:

1—Indigo Bunting
2—Adult male Purple Finches
3—Juncos
4—Adult White-throated Sparrows
5—Song Sparrows
6—White-crowned Sparrows
7—Immature White-throated Sparrows
8—Immature Purple Finches
9—Chipping Sparrows

Indigo Bunting

Only a single male came, three days in succession, but at his arrival and with consistent offensive behavior, he cleared the rock of all other birds for as long as he wished to feed.

Adult Male Purple Finches

Three of these, one in full color, had the rock to themselves whenever they desired. Females and immature of their own species were driven off together with the others. When the least full-plumaged male was alone, two females often disputed the rock.

Junco

Snowbirds were third in the list of tyrants.

Adult White-throated Sparrows

These were next in dominance but often permitted the others to feed around the edges of the seed manna.

Song Sparrows

These smaller birds almost always drove off the larger White-crowned.

White-crowned Sparrows

Three adults gave way before the Song Sparrows and the adult White-throats but bullied the immature of the latter.

Immature White-throated Sparrows

Seldom did one or more feed in tolerance with the adults.

Female and Immature Purple Finches

These could never be sure of uninterrupted feeding when any of the other five species were about.

Chipping Sparrows

These were at the bottom of the scale of tolerance, but they suffered no lack of feeding opportunity, for they were so tame that they were the first to return after human interference.

Neither size nor abundance of individuals had anything to do with this order of tolerance. If we consider the sequence from dominant to submissive as 1 to 9, we find the corresponding order in respect to size, from the smallest up, to be: 9,1,3, 2,8,5,4,7 and 6. The same scale in abundance to rarity is: 1, 6,4,9,5,3,7 and 8.

Temporary shifts in dominance order was occasioned by the individuality of some single bird. One Song Sparrow fought steadily for his rights with all above him, and one immature Purple Finch had to be physically assaulted before he would give way.

When eight or ten immature Purple Finches occupied the rock there was no uncertain evidence of intra-specific order of dominance, but they all looked so much alike that casual efforts to distinguish between individuals were futile.

It is interesting to note that numbers one and two in the scale of dominance, Indigo Bunting and Purple Finch males, are the only ones with brilliant colors."

Thank you, Dr. Beebe.

There was a local legend that a buckwheat field would attract birds, so Elmer bought a small plough second hand, which would follow Old John, borrowed a harrow, and broke about an acre of ground which had gone to inferior hay behind the plant house. There we put in a few more rows of potatoes, beets and sweet corn, with the rest in buckwheat. As it was outside the charged wire, the deer kept the beets mowed down to invisibility, and the potatoes in newly turned ground were nothing to brag about. But we ate corn till it almost came out of our ears, and we had a lot left over. The birds gathered too, for the buckwheat. Every time you approached the field they rose from it like a cloud of flies, but there were no new species attracted which were not already on the list. Che-Wee enjoyed bouquets of the half-ripe buckwheat stalks, and there was not enough seed left by his friends and relations to be worth harvesting. Still, everybody had a picnic all summer long, and that was the main idea.

Tree swallows will use bluebird houses, and are much more fun, as they almost die of curiosity at everything that goes on in human affairs near by. We put a bird-house on the balsam tree on the south lawn and then were afraid it was too near the porch. But the tree swallows moved in at once and the more we ate on the porch and sat in chairs on the lawn beneath the tree the better they liked it, and the bird which was doing its turn of duty on the eggs would practically lean its elbows on the edge of the hole to watch us, like a lady at a tenement window.

Will mentioned one day that white feathers are something no nest-building swallow can resist, and said they would go miles to find white chickens to get a lining for the nest. So I snipped open an old bed pillow, and we all spent a hilarious hour sitting on a bank above the vegetable garden where there is another house on a pole which had been chosen by another pair of tree swallows who were just then setting up house-keeping. It was a bright windy day and we would let single white feathers flutter from our fingers on to the wind and watch the birds swoop and catch them in midair. Feathers that escaped them were so precious that the swallows would light on the ground within a few feet of us to capture them. It must have been a beautiful nest, and unusually soft.

By midsummer we were simply creeping with chipmunks, which were inevitably attracted by the birdseed, and after all they didn't know it wasn't meant for them. I can bear to have woodchucks shot, as they are fat, sluggish, greedy, unappeal-ing creatures and can wreck a small garden in one invasion—if only they wouldn't sit up with their little front paws held against their chests! But chipmunks are cute. They have big trustful eyes, and neat little striped bodies, and their move-ments are quick and gay, and they scold like fury if you tres-pass on their chosen ground. You can respect chipmunks, they are getting something out of life. But they go too far. They not only steal the birdseed, they raise enormous families and wean them on our strawberries.

The strawberry and asparagus bed is separate from the rest of the garden and lies on a terrace at the back of the rock garden. Cheesecloth strips stretched across the top of twelve-inch chick-wire will keep the birds out of ripe strawberries—most of them, anyway—but not the chipmunks. They go over or under any sort of fencing and they don't even wait for the berries to ripen, they simply nip through the stems of *all* the berries and leave the green ones on the ground. We weren't getting one good berry for the table. It is easy—too easy—to pick off a chipmunk with a .22, but I am squeamish. Elmer had to be called on to leave his beloved "woodin' " with the tractor and devise a humane Operation Chipmunk for the strawberry bed.

He ran a wire from the main electric fence around the four small posts at the corners of the bed which supported the chick-fencing, and joined it to the fencing at intervals. The charge would be less than the deer got, but we thought it would be enough. The chipmunks would come along in the wet morning grass and put their paws or their nose against the fence, and bingo. It happened just that way. One morning a chipmunk was seen to sail through the air in a parabola a yard high and land on the cheesecloth in the middle of the bed, like a trapeze artist in the life-net. It didn't kill him, because we never found his body among the strawberry plants. But he was never seen thereabouts again as far as I know, and we had a fair crop from then on.

When the new refrigerator actually arrived it caused almost as much excitement as the furnace had done. It was the bottled-gas type, as electric refrigerators are too hard on light plants, and it was so big the kitchen door had to be taken off to admit it. It had a frozen-foods compartment, for the storage of packaged vegetables, fruits, and meats, along with a generous supply of ice cubes. If I had not learned to take Elmer's advice, even against my own inclinations, I would have missed owning what has become an indispensable convenience. The frozen-foods compartment adds to the original cost of the refrigerator, and I was in an economical mood, inclined to consider any ordinary ice-making refrigerator a sufficient blessing without any additional gimmicks like frozen foods.

But one of Elmer's pre-war jobs was refrigerators, and rather grudgingly I ordered the model he recommended, and now we couldn't live without it. The fact that a twice-weekly frozen-foods delivery service has since put in an appearance along our road isn't the only reason. A supply of chops or steak brought back from town, rewrapped in freezing paper, and tucked away next the ice-trays will freeze itself and keep indefinitely. An ice-cream carton of unsugared strawberries or raspberries frozen will last Che-Wee for treats long after the outdoor season has passed. And these experiments have roused in me a still unfulfilled desire for a small deep freeze. Only here I am handicapped by the Kohlers. A freezing mechanism simply works them too hard. They could handle it, but the wear and tear is considerable.

Never buy a new refrigerator without that freezing compartment, even if you live in town. The satisfaction of being able to store away the makings of a few meals in advance in case of emergency, bad weather, ill health, or sudden laziness about going out to the shops is unbelieveable. I have already admitted there must have been a squirrel somewhere in my family tree.

The refrigerator brought with it on the same bottled-gas hook-up what had by then become to me the ultimate symbol of domestic luxury—automatic hot water. They put a new water tank in the cellar with gadgets on it, such as an aquastat, and the installation man lighted the gas. When the water reaches 145° something turns off everything but a pilot light—when enough water is drawn to lower the temperature something turns the gas on again, briefly, until it is restored—nobody goes near it—all the dishwater we want—all the hot baths we want—no more cellar stairs—no more fires to build

—now we could really relax. Even the change over from the empty gas cylinder to the spare is practically automatic. All I have to do after the indicator on the gauge has swung to *Reserve* is send off a printed prepaid postcard and a new cylinder arrives by truck like magic. Once more the happy chant was heard: *Worth every penny of it!*

And as a sort of postscript to this bottled-gas job, we got a small two-burner tabletop stove, which was installed on a cabinet beside the oil-burner range, and which boils a kettle or fries a chop much more quickly than the range and does not heat up the kitchen on a warm summer day.

Next, the small boys were eliminated by a power lawn-mower, painted bright orange, with a ridiculous little motor which starts by a cord, like an outboard. It cost not much more than one summer's wages for our little helpers, and it is always there when wanted, requires only gasoline to make it work, and accomplishes in a single morning what took all day before. It has to be guided, of course, but it does all the rest, and operating it is largely a matter of learning to give it its head. If you try to help it it takes charge and drags you around. At low speed, on a sweep of lawn, it is gentle enough for a lady. On steep slopes or narrow paths it needs a firm hand. It doesn't like nails or wire or rocks in the grass, otherwise it gives no trouble, mechanically. If it does strike something the blades can't cut, it throws out a little pin and sits there patiently till you put a new one in. A child could do it.

I was trailing contentedly along behind it on the vast back lawn one hot sunny morning, deafened to everything but the sound of its motor, when I came to the end of a row, turned, and saw a respectable-looking station wagon standing in the road just short of the barn, waiting for me to discover its arrival. I greeted the man behind the wheel and strolled over to him. He gave his name, called me by mine, and asked if I would sell the hay standing.

His white shirt was very clean, his long New England jaw was freshly shaven, and I liked him at once. It was almost with regret that I said the hay was already arranged for. His manner was so relaxed and friendly, one farmer to another, that I felt free to consult him on the matter which was uppermost in our minds just then—a side-delivery rake, second-hand. He didn't know of one. But he had a couple of possibilities. Then, as we intended to fertilize after the hay was cut, I asked him about manure, and he told me where some might be for sale. We went on chatting, he leaning on the wheel, myself against the car, while his sky blue gaze travelled appreciatively over my fields and woods beyond the barnyard.

He said it was good hay. He said it was a pretty place. I liked him still more for praising it. So I heard myself saying to this stranger that I had got all caught up now in the idea of bringing it back a little, treating it right, making the most of it, instead of regarding it as just a summer home. This wasn't bragging, or asking for kudos—it was just a friendly impulse to let him know that the place wasn't wasted on me, and that I meant to do what I could for it. His eyes came back to me with a singularly direct and searching look. "I wish a lot of other people felt the way you do," he said. "I just wish they did."

His simplicity and conviction went straight home to the thing inside me that was turning into a farmer. It made me feel good. It disposed of any last lingering uncertainties. I felt elected. Although I shall probably never see him again, we parted friends.

When Elmer came and I told him about the visitor I was still feeling good. Mixed with my gratification was some surprise that the little I was trying to do had seemed to make so much impression. But Elmer was only surprised that I was surprised. Nothing is too little to do for the land. He thought I knew that.

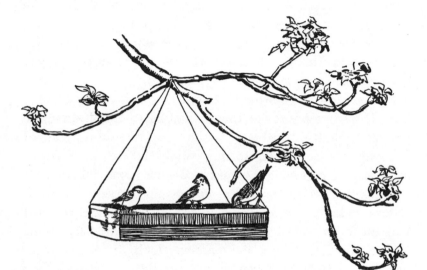

11.

*I*N 1947 FOR THE FIRST
time the hay was our own affair, to be harvested and sold as a
product of the place, like the syrup. Heretofore it had been
sold standing, for what amounted to not much more than a
dollar a ton, to people who had the equipment to cut it and
an immediate use for it, and it had evidently yielded them a
tidy profit over the expense involved. We could not expect a
profit for some time, above the purchase of our own equipment and the annual hiring of extra labor for haying week.
But even if we never any more than broke even between the
cost of harvesting and the sale price, I would still have preferred to do it ourselves without depending on outsiders. We

hoped that we could do better than that—much better than that if we fertilized at once—so that within a few years we should not only be able to pay for the equipment out of the returns but show a margin of profit each year ourselves. I was quite willing to wait for it to catch up with itself in this way, for the sake of making the place more self-contained and self-supporting.

We bought a new John Deere mowing-machine for around $145, the horse-drawn model. The rubber-tired, tractor-drawn variety, which cost much more, was also still scarcer than side-delivery rakes—if it was possible for anything to be scarcer than those. It is doubtless plain by now that Elmer like Kipling's Mr. Bivvens is a man-of-infinite-resource-and-sagacity, and he contrived for the mower an ingenious Rube-Goldberg cable-and-lever hook-up to Old John's rear, so that its cutter-bar could be raised and lowered by him while riding in the tractor seat, instead of having to be operated by someone in the seat carried by the mower itself. This took time but was important, as the fields are stony and rough in spots and the cutter-bar must be capable of skimming easily over the top of obstructions. If it hits a stone it damages some tooth-guards or snaps the Pitman-rod or cracks the shoe. Everybody expects to break a Pitman-rod every so often anyway. Elmer always keeps at least one spare in the barn, and patiently replaces the broken one when necessary. Starr Cooper's horse-drawn mower wears a cracked one splinted together with tape, which is alleged to work better than it did before—has a little give to it, you might say. Could be.

One thing I like about the people I have encountered in Vermont is an absence of bad temper with inanimate objects. This is not to subscribe in any way to the growing popular impression that the whole population of the state oozes a particular brand of Yankee humor and charm. I imagine that for its size Vermont produces just about as many unlikable people as any other state in the union, and I may only have been fortunate in my associations. The local breed is a pretty pure strain of Anglo-Saxon from the original British settlers, its vocabulary is rich and broad, its speech slow and quiet, its humor enigmatic, and its manners are innately good. On the other hand our Elmer is straight French Canadian, and exactly the same characteristics prevail in him, except that he even underplays the Yankees with an ease and skill which many an actor would give his eyeteeth to learn.

It may be too that anywhere on the land, away from the perpetual exasperated hustle of cities, people are more tolerant of delay and frustration. Anyway, I have noticed many times that when something breaks or balks there is seldom any language or banging things about—rather a resigned sort of curiosity as to the worst that has happened, and a humorous contest of ingenuity against cussedness in the mending of it. Probably this appeals to me because Will and I both so consistently and futilely fight the non-human obstinacy of things like can-openers and automatic elevators and taxi-doors, and as consistently come off second-best. In the country there is a cheerful sort of oh-you-would-would-you attitude which saves a lot of nervous wear and tear.

We got a rubber-tired second-hand wagon for $35, also designed to be horse-drawn, but Elmer altered the tongue to suit Old John and built a wide hay-rack body from a stack of old lumber under the barn, and we hoped that with careful driving it would last out the season, which it did.

The baler engaged for this year was operated by two brothers who ran an up-to-date farm and occasionally hired out their equipment with driver—the fee based on the number of bales accomplished, not the number of hours spent on the place. A baling machine is a Golem-like monster, bright red, towering above the tractor which hauls it. With a relentless, intelligent efficiency it travels slowly along the windrows scraping up the hay neatly off the ground into its maw. It cuts, compresses, and ties it with string into oblong bundles weighing fifty to sixty pounds each, which are passed rearward down a sort of gangway and spilled off on to the ground again at regular intervals. Worse still, *it counts them for you* as it goes, and rings them up on a little gauge. You ask the *baler* how many it has done, not the driver, and it always knows. Frightening. Rather like Charlie McCarthy, who when Edgar Bergen dies is sure to go right on talking, unassisted.

But if the baler has a super-human authority, the side-delivery rake, which we hired along with it, gives an impression of gibbering metal insanity. Its hind wheels are undersized and misplaced, its long, mobile teeth create a dervish dizziness, the noise it makes is a maniacal chatter—and yet out of this mechanical delirium emerge the neat, snaky windrows of gleaming hay which guide the baler from end to end of the field in a serene, continuous, time-saving pattern. It is an art to rake for the baler, so that by deviations and kinks in the windrows the man who follows on the baler tractor is warned of hidden rocks and holes in time to avoid them with his own far more temperamental machine. When a baler breaks down it breaks down all over everything, the ground roundabout becomes strewn with intricate innards and tools, parts have to be sent away for, and they sometimes take so long arriving that meanwhile the weather goes to pieces out of sympathy, and hay which was dried and raked is soaked with untimely showers and has to be tedded and raked again, or with bad luck becomes a total loss.

Farmers are said to be always at war with the weather, but nothing so reduces you to your proper size in the universe as the annual effort at haying time to anticipate and take advantage of and guard against the mysterious, uncaring, inexorable changes from wet to dry and back again. The baler man sends word that he will start on your place on Thursday and to let down four or five acres at once. Then the sky clouds over. The radio says showers. Do you heed the baler schedule, which is always crowded, and take a chance on mowing, or do you heed the weather bureau and hold back?

If the baler comes and you have nothing ready cut and raked he may remark callously that he can't bale hay when it's standing up, and take on some other job first, and you must wait your turn again. Or you may shut your eyes to the cloudy sky and mow, and then it pours rain and the baler doesn't come anyhow, and your hay is wet. It can get wet once, after it is cut, and be tedded over and dry out and be raked again and baled. It can't stay wet or get wet twice and be worth much. And it shouldn't get wet at all after it is baled. This means that more than once I have driven Old John, hauling the laden wagon with two or three men pitching bales on to it, until it was almost too dark to see a tractor length ahead. We have promised him a headlight for next year.

Our 1947 crop paid for the baler hire and the mower and the labor—or, otherwise, it paid for the fertilizer and spreader which we bought in preparation for next year. If we had not bought fertilizer we should have broken even on actual harvest cost the first year. With the fertilizer we meant to increase our yield by half for next year and thus put something back on our investment. We have no cattle, and the hauling of manure so raises the cost that it is not practical to use any quantity of it. We had samples taken of the soil, and ordered a potash, nitrogen, super-phosphate mixture which was put on as the ground froze that autumn.

Though our fields had not been fertilized or limed since heaven knew when, the hay was better than I had been led to believe by its former purchasers. This year's crop was bought from us for $30 a ton and sold again by the local feed store, and the story is that it made such a hit with the cows to whom it was fed that their owner at once put in a bid for our next year's crop. I never knew before how discriminating cows are. It seems that these considered our hay good to the last wisp. With other hay there were likely to be leavings. We only hoped that the fertilized product next year wouldn't upset them.

12.

AS SOON AS THE HAY IS
in the barn you start thinking about next year's sugaring.
There is always more wood to bring down—fifteen to twenty
cords of it. There are always buckets to paint, if you have any
wooden ones, always repairs and improvements to be made
around the sugar-house. Our wooden buckets had leaked
badly the first year, but most of them could have their hoops
tightened and with a new coat of paint inside and out be good
for several years more. A lot of young trees that had never
been tapped at all were going to waste, and we could use twice
as many buckets anyway. We compromised on five hundred
new metal ones, which never require painting, and with the

order signed away our syrup earnings for the coming year. There were no complaints from me. The sap could not be gathered without buckets to hold it. Once the buckets are owned, it costs very little more to set fifteen hundred than a thousand, but the eventual returns are half again as much. Profit on this place was always intended to wait on productiveness.

This brings me again to that autumn day with which the book begins—when I painted buckets by myself in the barn, and knew for a few minutes an elusive, illuminating joy in the whole undertaking. I stood then definitely committed, and I was glad. The new buckets had been spoken for, and the fertilizer was in the barn, waiting to be spread. A second gasoline tank had been buried behind the plant house so that over a thousand gallons could be stored—a full winter's supply and more, as it was impossible for even the Flying Red Horse to negotiate the lane which led to the tanks once the winter snow set in. A thousand-gallon tank for furnace oil had been buried beside the drive to simplify that delivery as well, replacing the two two-hundred-and-seventy-fives which had been in the cellar.

During the coming winter before sugaring time began Elmer was to finish the insulation job upstairs and make some repairs to the dining-room ceiling, which showed signs of coming down. (This proved to be because some genius in times past had sawed the main stringer of the house practically through for the introduction of a stove-pipe, long since removed, and the last remaining charred edges of the beam had finally given way, so that the guest-room floor was resting mainly on the lath of the dining-room ceiling. Things you don't know when you buy a house.)

The woodshed lean-to with its aluminum roof had been added to the sugar-house to keep the wood dry, and was already half full of tidily piled logs and slab wood, cut into lengths with the power-saw which ran off Old John with a belt—a job to which Will had bent a willing but unaccustomed back. T-20 had his winch now, and was to have a small snow-plough or pusher of his own when Elmer got round to make it out of half a gasoline barrel.

The winch, which came from Sears Roebuck and cost about $150, was a new bright blue, and T-20 was an old bright red. The power take-off cost about $40, and a few hours work by Elmer at the village garage attached them to T-20's rear. The result was efficient, but a trifle gaudy. Nothing, however, impairs T-20's stolid dignity.

During one of those few days I spent alone with Che-Wee, three misguided youths chose to hold up a diner in a nearby town and shoot a policeman who interfered. They got away with the contents of the cash register and their guns, and were believed to be headed this way, on foot or hitch-hiking, probably pretty reckless and frightened, and a general alarm went out on the radio. I, in my happy isolationist mood, was not listening to the radio news, and Elmer's telephone call that evening came out of a clear sky. He had been stopped on the way home by some of his buddies in the State Police, who were searching all cars, and they advised him not to let me stay alone on the place that night, but to move me out entirely. They had caught one boy, wounded in the fight, but the other two were still at large, and if anyone chose to cut my telephone wire and take possession of the house I might possibly have a rather lively time. I was inclined to argue the probability, from my persistent delusion of owning a citadel, but Elmer told me firmly that I must pack an overnight bag and ask the Coopers to drive me down to the inn in the village, and he would collect me there on his way in the next morning.

The Coopers, who had not listened to the radio either, backed him up emphatically when acquainted with the facts by telephone. When they drove up to fetch me—it was already dark, and there was just that moment when in spite of myself I looked to see if the car was theirs—I had my bag ready, and in another one beside it was Che-Wee, routed out of his sleeping-cage and bundled into his travelling-cage, and pretty disgruntled about it, but he wasn't going to be left to any bandits if I wasn't there.

The inn is a cosy place, whose hostess I already knew, and I was made welcome, given a big front bedroom with a wood fire in it, and invited into the kitchen for a friendly cup of tea. There was not much business at that time of year, and the only other guests were an elderly couple who soon went up to bed. She couldn't close up because a man who had reserved a room had not yet arrived, though there was an atmosphere of general drawing in and locking up throughout the village as the hunt went on; arrangements were being made for her son's girl friend, whose parents were away, to spend the night with friends instead of staying at home alone, and she lived right in the village at that.

We were still in the kitchen over the tea and bread and jam, a very sleepy Che-Wee being made much of in his cage on the sink-board, when the front door opened quietly and she said with some relief, "There he is! Now we can lock up." But it was part of the posse, the town manager, no less, a tall, competent guy with revolvers sticking out here and there, who wanted to use the telephone. He conducted a long, cryptic, rather grim conversation with his sheriff, to which we listened shamelessly and made very little of it. When he hung up he asked, innocently, for there is no public dining-room at that inn, where he could get a cup of coffee as everything in the village was shut. We said we would make him some right there. It was cold, and getting late, and he hesitated. He had a policeman outside, he said, who was just as done up as he was, they had been at it for hours— Bring in your policeman, we said, and the coffee pot went on and the electric toaster came out.

It was one of those things. They sat down wearily at the kitchen table with its fresh checked cloth and went to work on the coffee and buttered toast and jam. The policeman was a fine piece of Hollywood type casting, large, leonine, in dark blue uniform with black gaiters and Sam Browne, slung round with revolvers. Their conversation was terse and tough and humorous. The wounded boy was in bed at the jail, not very comfortable—they saw no reason why he should be too comfortable—and was not talking, *yet*. One of the other two seemed to have thumbed a ride in this direction and might be anywhere, and all the towns and bus stops were being watched like mouseholes. That was about all we got out of them, and they soon departed, walking rather stiffly still, but very grateful and polite.

I found it difficult to settle down to sleep after all this, but I wrapped Che-Wee's cage in my woollen robe, for the bedroom was getting cold and the grate fire was out, left the window closed on his account, and got into bed with a book. There was even a reading-light, nicely placed. I did sleep. I breakfasted early in the spotless kitchen, introduced Che-Wee to various well-wishers who came into the gift-shop which is part of the inn, and went out into a bright crisp morning to meet Elmer's car.

We have our own small still unsolved mystery to contribute. The barn doors, which were closed when Elmer left before dark, were two feet open when we drove into the yard that morning. The barn was full of baled hay, and I had rather an odd moment to see him walk into it, silhouetted against the light. Nobody was there, of course. Either a searching party or a fugitive—or a deer, for all we'll ever know!—had moved the doors. The boys were both rounded up by the police that day, and no further harm was done.

But it brought up again the matter of a dog. There are objections to having a dog, strange as that may seem to some people. It might roll in the flower beds, it might scare the birds away from the feeders, it might snap at Che-Wee, it would have to be left behind whenever I go to New York—although I don't fool myself that any dog which went to live with Elmer and his two little hounds in my absence would miss me much. (He says there is always room for one more dog at his house, which with his wife's spaniel already has three.) The question arises as to how much good a dog would be against a man with a gun who really meant business, and the dog is supposed to be still ahead, if it has been trained to handle men with guns. It would also have to be trained to stay off my chintz slip-covers, but that is far from impossible. Above all, it would have to understand about Che-Wee, who is inclined to potter about on the floor and who would never have the sense to keep out of its reach. I am assured that it could even be trained to let him ride on its back, which I am quite willing to believe, but the actual training seems to me to involve a certain amount of risk at which I boggle. The problem of what kind of dog is also good for a lot of discussion—big enough to be a protection, not too big to come in the house, and what about its food. . . .

Dog people are always amazed at such vacillation on my part, and no doubt very impatient too. They will think still less of me when I admit that I have a standing offer of a well-bred Doberman puppy from good kennels whenever I care to claim one, and yet another offer from a man who breeds collies. But it's not so simple as all that. I still have no dog. There haven't been any more hold-ups, either. And a little to my own surprise, that brief flurry has in no way affected my perhaps imbecile sense of security on my own land.

I am beginning to believe that houses are people, with personalities that are lovable or not, and auras that are noticeable even to those of us who are not psychic. Life in this house in Vermont is, I suppose, complicated by personal anxieties and tensions as numerous and acute as in most households. Nobody here is without faults and bees in the bonnet, nobody is particularly saintly, the daily domestic road is not magically paved. And yet—everyone who comes here seems to experience a smoothing-out and cheering-up which breeds sound sleep and good appetite and a happier state of mind than they brought with them. This *dolce far niente* effect seems to me to be not entirely owing to the mountain air, the wide view, the absence of hurry and crowds—nor to the presence of the by no means celestial hosts. I think it is the place. I think there is benevolence here, in the *genius loci*. I think we have a good fairy. I think the house itself gives out good will and comfort.

It need not always have been so ever since it was built, roundabout 1840. A house can resent its inhabitants, I think, so that things go consistently wrong for them in it. I am beginning to believe that a house, like people, can choose its friends. This one was neglected and misused for years before we took it. It had been sold to the sort of city folk who lived in it only a few weeks in each year, and only camped out in it when they were here. They had had its hay cut, after a fashion, but they gave it few repairs. Its own foundations, to say nothing of the barn and the sugar-house, were in a state of increasing decay. Atrophy was slowly setting in, and perhaps shame, until it was sullen and lonely and discouraged when we came. It seems to me to have responded in an almost human way to a little cherishing, and it wears a look of expectant tidiness and welcome now which may not be just because of a fresh coat of paint. . . .

13.

*I*T WAS PROBABLY DUE
as much to my own ignorance as to Elmer's habitual under-
statement that I was not sufficiently worried about the barn
when I left for New York that autumn.

I knew that we had a job to do there in the spring, of
course. I knew that the barn creaked alarmingly in the merest
breeze, that its south side had bulged way out of line, and that

the back doors—it stands on a slope, one story high in front, two at the back—swung crazily level with the ground without even a sill, much less a foundation, on that side. I knew that the weight of the handsome slate roof, added at no doubt great expense by somebody not long before we bought the place, had caused the whole thing to buckle foolishly at the knees, and that the rotting wooden props underneath it had always been too few and too far between. But I didn't realize that, in words of one syllable, the barn was just about ready to fall down in a heap.

It was a bad winter with a lot of snow, and a recurrent strep throat infection prevented me from running up to Vermont for a few days after Christmas as I had intended. I didn't see the barn again, nor give it much thought, until Will had taken off for another expedition to Venezuela and sugaring time had come round again.

I don't know if you remember now about the spring of 1948. It was then that the Berlin airlift began. And it was exactly ten years after the Germans moved into Vienna. There is a silly superstitious something about a neat anniversary like that. Why ten years should be any more significant than nine or eleven makes no sense, but I had been aware of the same sort of thing in 1934, twenty years after the beginning of the Other War, when in October the assassination of King Alexander at Marseilles sent a chill down our spines in London because of June, 1914, when the Austrian Archduke had died at Sarajevo.

So in the spring of 1948 I carried with me a brooding, fatalistic memory of March, 1938, which was before Munich, mind you, and long before Prague. It was Austria then, too, and colorless, defenceless, bedevilled Schuschnigg, unhappy successor to the murdered Dolfuss who had been allowed by his

Nazi captors to bleed to death slowly on a sofa in his own Chancellory. . . . Schuschnigg, summoned to Berchtesgaden and given a paper to sign, or else. Schuschnigg's last radio message to his people, ending with that hoarse, broken prayer. . . . When Hitler took Vienna in 1938 I had already booked passage for my annual summer in England, and I went, and I was there at the time of Munich. And it seemed fantastic, in 1948, that a whole war had been fought and presumably won since then, and that now again from Berlin the miasma rose of conflict and hatred and double-double-dare.

It has been hinted since then that the international scene was even darker than we were allowed to realize at the time, but it looked bad enough. Germans or Russians, the threat was the same, the methods were the same, the running sore was still Berlin. And next time would be worse. Each time it is necessarily worse. It was very easy to get into one of those where-will-it-*end* depressions early in 1948, especially as Will's obstinate commonsense—too obstinate, too rational, last time, for unfolding events, but very tonic all the same—was not within my daily reach. And I began to take with even greater seriousness than before the task of making an adequate, comfortable, partly self-supporting home for half a dozen people, if need be, of the country house.

We migrated again with Che-Wee in April, to put things in order for the summer, and I had with me as usual the interlined manuscript of a book to finish for autumn publication. As we drove up the muddy road I noticed a stout beam, an eight by eight, propping up the south side of the barn where the worst bulge was. Elmer led me down underneath and unfolded a heartrending story of his below-zero struggles to keep the thing on its feet at all when the wind blew. Temporary braces and blocking up were everywhere visible now, and I gathered that he had spent most of the winter down there, holding up the barn by main force and prayer. His estimate of the cost of saving it now was steep, but it couldn't be built again for many times that sum, and there had to be a place to store the hay crop and house the machinery. So I ordered 1200 cinder blocks, 8 x 12 x 16, to build a new foundation, and lumber of all descriptions, and the work was to begin immediately after sugaring was out of the way—or we wouldn't be ready in time for hayin'.

Meanwhile the sap was running.

To stand in the middle of the sugar-bush and hear the musical drip of the sap into metal buckets and gauge the wealth of the flow by the tempo of the drops is perennially exciting, even to men who have sugared all their lives. The air is balmy but fresh, the ground under your feet is wet and snowy, the buds have not yet begun to swell—when the buds come, sugaring is over, because the sap turns dark and strong. But the smell and the surge and the *sense* of spring are in your nostrils and in your veins. The year has turned. Warmth and color and harvest are on the way.

For people who have always lived in cities, bound on the wheel, doing much the same sort of work every month in the year, their trend of thought not much affected by the change of seasons, country life has a surprising continuous novelty. It is supposed to be the other way round. Variety is alleged to reside in town, dullness and sameness and boredom in the countryside. It doesn't work out that way.

At the beginning of the year everything is concentrated on sugaring. No inside work, short of emergency, nothing anywhere that can wait, takes precedence over the absorbing business of collecting the last few cords of wood, breaking out the sugar-roads, readying the sugar-house and the gathering equipment, so that when that thaw comes, and the weather is right, and the sap begins to run, there will be no delay. At the end of the short season, all the gear has to be cleaned and put away in good order, and that is no small job either. Next, everything revolves around the planting, even with a small garden like ours where things are grown only for the table. Sorting the seeds, deciding the layout, feeling the soil, watching the weather, plowing, sowing, cultivating, cutting pea-brush, supporting the tomatoes. . . . Haying, which comes after that, demands most of all, it always seems; sharpening the knives of mowing-machine and scythes, checking up on the tractors, arranging for the baler, committing yourself to an approximate date, and then as that date approaches seizing the right morning to begin cutting and raking, getting the baler there on time after all, getting the baled hay into the barn before dark clouds can burst. . . . It is all single-minded, undistracted, jealous devotion to the project in hand, so that you think, talk, eat, sleep, and *dream* nothing but sugar, or planting, or hay—and always and forever, *the weather*. Writing a book is the only undertaking I know that is comparable to farming for preoccupation, unless it is the actor's consuming agony in a new part. It is monotonous only very briefly. Then the travail changes its whole aspect, but not its intensity. And in 1948, there was added to the usual inexorable list our own private lowering bother about the The Barn.

Sugaring had us now, though, to the exclusion of everything else. You watch the sun and the clouds and the wind and the thermometer. One day there is a certain whiff in the air. The dreigh goes round with the bucket towers, and the roads get a final going over. The next round taps the trees on the lower slope, near the house, and sets the buckets and the covers there, and the beautiful *drip, drip, drip* begins. For round number three the gathering-tub is hoisted on to the dreigh and secured with logging chains, the shiny 20-quart gathering-pails are stacked in the screen trays which cover the openings in the top of the tub to sieve out leaves and twigs and occasional sap-happy insects. As the tractor pulls away from the barnyard the smoke of the first fire being kindled in the arch curls up from the sugar-house stack. With water in the pans, Elmer is checking for leaks and warming up the arch. There is a visible difference in the look of boiling water and boiling sap, so when the first load of sap begins to flow from the storage tank through the hose and the back pan towards the front pan and the draw-off faucet, the water is drained off ahead of it.

To ride on the dreigh and watch the heavy buckets of sap lifted shoulder high and poured through the strainers into the gathering-tub—it foams like beer—to feel the increasing tug of the heavy tub on the tractor as it nears its eight-barrel capacity—to watch the easy, unhurried, systematic movements of the men from tree to tree, and listen to their casual, salty remarks as they work—to hear the roar of the tractor engine up hill and the slosh and gurgle of the sap in the tub, splashing up cold through the wire netting into your face if you peer in at the rising tide as you lurch along between stops—that's the fun of sugaring for me.

Snow-fleas mean a thaw and a good run. There are a variety of small, purposeful tracks in the snow beside the road, and the men know them at a glance for deer, racoon, mice, rabbit, fox, sometimes the big pad of a bob-cat—they say that when a bob-cat jumps a deer's neck the deer always makes for scrub pine to try and brush it off, but seldom succeeds or survives. I have still not learned the maze of turns in the upper circles of the sugar roads and probably never will, but land-marks emerge as time goes on. You could go round and round up there until you dropped or starved to death and never be off a nice road that looks as though it will surely lead *some-where*, but the pattern makes sense to the men who have de-signed it so that they need never back or turn or retrace their steps with the tub.

I was lucky enough to be there the day the runner broke. We were high up on the back lot, about as far from home base as we could be, with the tub nearly full, when it happened. We were still using a rather light horse-sled—all we had been able to find in a hurry the first year—behind T-20, whose twenty-six horse-power waits for nothing. We had new help this year, the best we ever had—greying, poker-faced Leon, even-tempered and humorous, and a husky kid of seventeen named Phil, untalkative and business-like, who took his sugar-ing seriously and worked at a sort of dog-trot and was worth his weight in syrup any day. We were moving on, between stops, Leon driving, Phil riding the tub, Elmer and myself walking close behind, when Phil gave a shout and pointed down. T-20 stopped in his tracks, Leon climbed out of the seat, Phil slid to the ground, and Elmer and I ranged along-side. The left runner had wrapped itself around a stone and snapped clean in two, with the metal shoe sticking out at an angle.

We all stood a moment like the Angelus, looking down. Then Leon said, "We-ell, it's better'n a broken leg," and El-mer sighed cheerfully and said, "We don't make much money, but we have a lot of fun. Gimme that ax."

Tranquil, patient, efficient, they cut and made a splint, and chained it to the runner. Before we had gone very far, nursing it gently over the bumpy road, it came adrift and the shoe flew out and the sled stalled again. A chilly mist had begun to fall, and the day was fading fast, and underfoot was icy mud. With complete good humor, they cut another splint and lashed that in place and the slow crawl began again—down hill towards home.

Riding on the one healthy runner, holding to the lurching tub, spanked by wet evergreen boughs along the roadside, I marvelled again. Nobody swore, nobody hurried, nobody blamed anybody or anything—the sled was too light for the tractor—lucky it had lasted as long as it did—we were in the middle of a run, and it was essential to find another sled at once, or a lot of good sap would be ruined—I would be put to extra expense which we had hoped to postpone another year, and they were sorry about that—to find a sled suddenly in the midst of the sugaring season would not be easy—but they took it all in their stride, and by the time we reached the house they had decided where to telephone to ask about a second-hand sled at a farm whose owner had recently died.

The strange thing is, we got it—an old but larger and stouter one, at a reasonable price. It went to work the next day and presumably will last forever.

Then there was the time T-20 sank nose first into a mud-hole and buried himself so deep he could only be half-cranked when he unexpectedly stalled. Shovels—axes—patience—wise-cracks—the sled was unhooked, T-20 was persuaded to back off at an angle to it—hitched on again, and detoured. And there was the time he couldn't make the steep rise on the far side of a brook with his treads gripping only mud and ice in the brook bed and a loaded tub behind him—and they had to stop and cut saplings to make a sort of corduroy track for him. Again the sled was detached and when T-20 had made his way across to firm ground alone, they unwound ten yards of his winch cable, hooked it on to the sled and used the winch to pull the sled up to where it could be re-attached to T-20 by his draw-pin, and we ambled on again, remarking that there had better be a bridge there before the tub went that way next year. Three bridges, at least, on different roads, to be constructed from wood which grew near by, were on the summer program. (When The Barn was done.)

There is satisfaction too in watching from the sugar-house door while the tub comes back from its round up by the nearest brook. It may be a slack time just then, with the sap low in the storage tank and the fire slowed to keep the pans going till the new supply arrives. Elmer will be smoking a cigarette in a few moments of rare leisure—he does the boiling now, for his father died in the autumn after giving us a good start in the right direction. (Elmer uses the ladle as the Old Man taught him, to test the syrup at drawing-off time, letting the golden stream apron down from the lower edge and pulling the draw-cock at the exact moment the consistency is right. The hydrometer his father would have none of, as being less reliable than his own seasoned judgment, is now dropped into each batch before the pail is emptied into the settler—a mere modest gesture, as it always sinks neatly to the red line.) Myself and whatever guests may be on hand are draped on kegs and benches, sipping the half-boiled syrup dipped from the front pan in plastic mugs. Conversation may be about anything under the sun, even sugaring. At about twenty-minute intervals the syrup apron will form on the ladle held high above the steaming pan and then the solid golden rope of syrup flows from the cock into the bucket, which happens to stand where the late afternoon sunlight shines through the west windows of the sugar-house. We can our syrup after it is cold, though the argument about hot or cold sealing can go on forever, with something to be said for both.

When T-20's bumble and growl are heard in the distance everyone brightens—the last of the sap which seeps slowly down the hose to the back pan will stretch now, till Leon gets here with more. T-20 comes into sight and pauses on the slope above the brook—pauses again for the trees at the edge of the swamp—and once more for the young maples at the corner of the hayfield.

You stand with the fragrance and warmth of the boiling sap at your back and the outside air cool in your face, and estimate the run by the way they tip the tree buckets into the gathering pails, and the heft of those pails as they are carried from tree to tree. "The trouble with that kid," said Elmer thoughtfully as we looked on one day from a distance of a hundred yards, "—his buckets come up off the ground just as easy when they're full."

The sugar house sits at the bottom of a small hill, close against the slope. T-20 pulls the dreigh in along a road which rides the crest, and the sap flows down a hose from the tub into long wooden spouts and through a hole under the eaves into the storage tank inside. Returning to the sugar-house with a full tub, a little stiff and chilly, the thing to do is to drink a cup of the hot "sweet," which is supposed to be very good for your insides in the spring.

1948 was not what you could call a good sugaring year up our way. The sap was not sweet, and took fifty gallons to one of syrup, instead of the normal thirty-five or forty. Nobody knows the answer to this variation in sweetness, which occurs from year to year without rhyme or reason. It may have something to do with the weather, nearly everything has.

Anyway the season was short and a good many people got disgusted and pulled their buckets. Then there was another sharp freeze and a thaw, which brought a wonderful last run, with flavor. Leon was still around because of the barn, and it didn't cost anything, they pointed out, to let our buckets hang—so we were still doing business when that last run came, though we agreed with Starr Cooper when he remarked that we'd have to get our buckets in sometime before hayin', he should think. We made about sixty gallons of syrup on that last run, all alone in our glory.

14.

*T*HEN, JUST AS WE WERE
ready to take a long breath and really begin on The Barn, it
rained.

It rained and was so cold that the sap buckets, gathered and
stacked beside the sugar-house, could not be comfortably
washed and stored. It rained so that no outside or underneath
work could be done on that ever-lasting Barn. It rained so
that no ploughing or planting could be done anywhere. It
rained so that everybody almost went crazy. Farmers, the
story was, couldn't do a thing but pace the floor.

While we marked time on the weather we filled in by
insulating the north and west walls of the upstairs bathroom,

and built handsome mouseproof storage and hanging cup-boards in the unfinished attic space between Mother's room and the study on the south end. But finally, in sheer despera-tion, working in an icy, saturated atmosphere with a search-ing wind between the cracks, Elmer and Leon began rip-ping out the stalls, which were on the worst side of the barn where the bulge was—room for twelve cows, once—and the floor, and taking a vast tuck from front to back in the beams which held up the barn floor. They did this by cutting off the small end of the splice and making a new one, and then attached T-20 by his cable to a brace on the outer backside —the cable passed through a hole cut in the back wall—and pulled. When the splice was closed up again they had taken out about six inches of bulge—the east-to-west bulge—but then T-20 didn't dare let go till the foundation went in under the east end, and we couldn't use him for anything else for weeks. The north-to-south bulge couldn't be touched at all until the foundation was ready, and every time they drove a shovel into the ground where they wanted to put cement bases for the foundation and the cinder-block pillars, water filled the hole.

And still it rained.

The wet delayed us altogether roundabout a month on The Barn, and while the hay wasn't growing much—*Wet May, Good Hay*, my eye!—we did begin to worry about where it was going to be put if it ever was cut. Not a blade of it could go into the barn till the work there was done. But at last, when Leon had gone on to another job, the sun showed its face at in-tervals, and three new men and a cement-mixer arrived, and things began.

I shall never know just how it was done. Using hydraulic jacks under big eight-by-eights which were inserted as props at the rear and against the north-south bulge, they raised it still more and T-20 took up some slack on the cable. They removed the rotted sills and all the board work to a height of eight feet above the ground, and for days the southeast corner hung literally in midair. The remains of the old stone foundation, such as it was, were crumbling, and not fit to set the new cinder-blocks on, to say nothing of the weight of the barn itself with the slate roof. This meant that the old stone work had to be pointed up and brought to a new level-line. The space left between this new level and the bottom of the jacked-up barn was carefully calculated to fit twelve rows of blocks plus the seams and a fraction of leeway to allow for the jacking.

When they dug down to set their cement base for the new foundation where none existed at all on the east end, they struck a solid rock ledge which apparently runs all the way under the barn, and which the original builders might easily have made use of by going down a little further in the first place—and we would not have been doing what we had to do now. The trench was then filled with stone and cement on top of the rock ledge to form a base for the cinder-blocks, on which the big new 8 x 8 timber sills would rest.

The cinder-blocks were laid by hand in cement along most of the north side and around the end to where the center door would come, and when they had set, the north side was let down on to them. Then the same thing was done on the other side of the door space and all the way up the south side. Two 5/8 inch wire rope cables were stretched crosswise just below the floor, and fastened with 2-foot turnbuckles, pulling the barn together by its own walls and holding it in position. Finally the whole barn was allowed to subside gently the fraction of an inch to rest on its new foundation, and the jacks and props came away.

Eight square cinder-block pillars had been set on cement bases in a double row underneath, leaving a center aisle and spacious bays with windows, one of which acquired walls and a plank floor and bench and became a workshop. The rest of the bays serve as stalls for the equipment, with a lot of storage room at the far end. Some day there should be a cement floor. Big new sliding doors above cement and plank sills replaced the sagging derelicts which had swung crazily on rusty hinges before. All the window frames were rebuilt and repainted, and the windows reset, upstairs and down. And upstairs the overhead crossbeams were reinforced and a new double floor was laid.

During this last part of the job the fledgling barn swallows from the nests up in the cupola were getting ready to try their wings. Instead of being frightened out of their wits by the noise of the power-driven table-saw and several hammers going at once, whole families sat in fascinated rows on the rafters and watched the workmen below with an almost embarrassing interest, like kibitzers around a New York excavation, while outside the bluebirds raised a second brood in the birdhouse on the telephone pole just above the cement-mixer. The young either grew up with nerves of steel, or else are full of mechanically induced neuroses, we'll never know which.

Meanwhile Will had sent a check from Venezuela, out of sympathy, and the amount was so exhilarating that I decided to make him a present and fulfill our hitherto rather vague ambition to convert the space which had been stalls into one big Room With a View. This project soon grew into what the movies call a Production, and threatened to go on forever in the making. Shut off from the rest of the barn by a double door, insulated on all sides with rock-wool four inches thick against dust, damp, and cold, with walls and ceiling of rockboard, there emerged a room thirty-four feet by fourteen. It has four windows, facing south and east, one of them six feet by three plate glass, with a windowseat, framed by bookshelves. The big window looks out eastward towards the rising sun and moon, across the hayfield where the deer come to graze at twilight. To sit there is like facing the rail from a deck-chair at sea—you go into a peaceful sort of trance, and don't do any work or even any thinking at all. It is furnished with a convertible bed-divan, a couple of large work-tables, an old rocking-chair, a kerosene heater, and a lot of shelves—already filling up with books from somewhere—and mouseproof storage cupboards all across one end. And although it comes as near to being an extravagance as I have yet committed on the place, it is—yes, here we go again—worth every penny of it.

BOCA CHICA

MAIL BOX

15.

IN CASE ANYONE IS
wondering about Che-Wee—I hate the tactless surprise with
which some people say, "Is he still alive?"—he was right there,
busy and happy with his many personal affairs, taking his daily
bath in a glass pie-dish on the kitchen sink, singing his small,
sweet, wavering song, loftily ignoring *hoi polloi* which came

to the feeding stations outside the windows and beyond the screen of his back porch.

He was having his small adventures, too, such as the day he rushed in to see what was going on at the sink and skidded into a dishpan full of Lux suds—luckily only lukewarm as wool socks were being washed in it and not dishes. He went right down out of sight, and Mother scooped him out, held him under the cold tap, mopped him with a towel, and set him on his feet. He looked ghastly, wetter than a bird ever was before, and with his feathers stuck tight to his body seemed about the size of a hummingbird. But he shook himself briskly, and his irrepressible crest came up—*"Well,* seems I had a bath!" He spent the next half hour busily combing himself out and shaking himself dry. No ill-effects whatever, for Che-Wee, but Mother was close to prostration.

And then there was the day the frozen-foods man left a lot of new parcels to be stored away in the freezer compartment of the refrigerator, and I worked for several minutes rearranging things with the main door open, as I went to and from the table. When I had finished and left the kitchen, I soon noticed that Che-Wee was nowhere to be seen, and began to think back to where I had noticed him last—on top of the pantry door watching me while I was at the refrigerator. We searched the kitchen and the pantry, in the recurrent weary game of hide-and-seek during which he usually sits motionless and mute, seeming to enjoy the anxiety we are bound to feel. When discovered, and severely talked to, he is pleased and a little smug, and very ready with his kiss-picks.

Finally we opened the refrigerator door in a rather aimless, exasperated way. There sat Che-Wee on the top shelf, next to his orange-colored box of dates, somewhat fluffed out and surprised, but full of his dignity. He had been shut up in a beastly cold dark place, where he couldn't even see to eat, but there had been no fluttering and no panic. He had merely waited, more or less resigned to the stupidity of the people he lived with, sure that eventually somebody would come back and let him out. He had gone in there after his dates, as any sensible bird would have done, when my back was turned. Luckily they were not in the frozen-foods compartment, but his feet were icy when he stepped without any undue haste on to my proffered finger. Well, it's about time, was written all over him. In my contrition I gave him a hunk of date, and mixed him a rum-and-orange-juice bracer in a teaspoon. So far as I know he never even sneezed, but *I* had the shakes for an hour.

This episode recalls a snowy night two winters back, when Che-Wee and I arrived from Vermont at the Grand Central Station in New York, and were met by the Marster, cold and a mite disgusted at having to come out and fetch us in such weather. Che-Wee was in his little covered cage inside his zipper bag, and I suggested to Will that I would stay inside the door until he got a cab, so Che-Wee wouldn't get chilled. "*Chilled!*" snorted the ornithologist. "I wish *I* had feathers!" And I passed the time while I waited—inside—for the cab, speculating ignorantly on which kind of bird Dr. Beebe would be if he had feathers. It's something to go into sometime, with his confrères.

Since the publication of Che-Wee's book of memoirs, necessarily rather brief, and the reprint of an extract from it in the *Reader's Digest*, it has appeared in eight of their nine foreign language editions, including the Japanese, and his fan mail has exceeded anything I have ever achieved alone. The eight translations of his name, made phonetically, were enchanting. In Portuguese he was *Chigui*, in Danish *Kvi-vit*, in

Swedish *Tji-vitt*, and in French *Tchi-Ouîi*. (In French he was understood to say to himself at one point, "*Voyons, dîtes-moi, qu'est-ce que je vais faire de ça?*" which is exactly what he *would* have said to himself in French.) In Japanese, where his space is identifiable only because his picture appears there, the character which stands for his name is a total mystery.

Almost everybody, it appears, has once attempted to rear an orphan bird, and in some cases has succeeded, and they write to tell us of their own experiences. They send him pictures of themselves and their foundlings, they send him Christmas cards and presents, such as little boxes of piñon nuts and dried apple seeds. I never had such charming letters from such nice people as Che-Wee has won for me. He loves all his presents, and will go anywhere and do anything for a piñon nut—he can't crack them himself, but the sound of the shell breaking between my teeth is unmistakable to him, and he knows the box they are kept in and often sits on it wistfully, hinting. They are now his special treats, but he gets only one a day as they are very rich. For a long time he cherished a heart-shaped scrap of pale blue silk crochet with a chain-stitch tail to it, enclosed by a lady in Georgia who happened to learn that he played with bits of ribbon and string, dragging them about and tossing them into the air. His little blue silk heart has finally disappeared from my desk—disintegrated, no doubt, from hard use.

Midway of his book we mentioned that when he invented his card trick—which is to pick up in his beak and cast aside a card laid across a dish of food or a crumb of piñon nut—he used a pretty postcard view of Waikiki Beach which Grant Mitchell had sent back during a USO tour in the Pacific. In due course a copy of the book with Che-Wee's compliments reached Grant, who had returned to New York, and right back to our door came his idea of a trinket for a bird—a small shallow silver porringer engraved with Che-Wee's name and his own, and very suitable to eat seeds out of. We have spent a lot of effort since then in rescuing it from people who thought it was only an ashtray.

One of his prettiest souvenirs is a letterfold which carries on the front a reproduction in color of a Chinese painting of a decorative bird identifiable as a jay perched among apple-blossoms. The exquisite penmanship of the message inside describes the writer as one of "two elderly ladies." She thanks us for writing the book and confesses that "like Aeneas in the schoolboy's translation, we wept tears of great length when our daily occupation forced us to give up a robin fledgling of intelligence and character in order to secure for him a more attentive household."

A lady in California sent us pictures and the story of a mocking-bird named Chipper that she had raised on pellets of egg-yolk and mashed potato. He grew up to help her sew, and always sang lullabies as he fell asleep. In that gracious climate she was able to turn him outdoors at an early age, and when I last heard from her he was still living in the garden and singing his lullabies from the sycamore tree.

Unlike a New England rose-breasted grosbeak, who turned up in our mail last summer, Chipper doesn't ever come inside or light on people any more. Tweet the grosbeak was raised according to the book of rules—Che-Wee's—which its adopted parents happened to possess, and being of similar nature and habits it thrived on Che-Wee's diet. Tweet's family made a definite effort to equip her—they decided she was female, though baby grosbeak males have the same plumage as their mothers the first season—to equip her for independent life by "training" her to crack seeds and chase insects, and then they released her in the woods around their camp. But Tweet insisted on coming home nights, flying in through an open door when invited. She allowed anyone to pick her up, even strangers, and several times a day would reappear from her "freedom" to demand her usual baby food. This was rather embarrassing to her hosts, who didn't feel that their city home would be any place for her and hoped to see her safely on her way before they left the camp. They wrote to me, a most engaging letter, asking me "how to explain to her that she is a big girl now and on her own." Rather treed myself, I replied the best I could, that Che-Wee was all right indoors and loved it, but that this was something between them and Tweet, and very difficult to decide, as I knew from experience. At least she had found her wings and was a little weathered. It was all taken out of their hands, for one night Tweet just didn't come home to bed, and was never seen again. I understood so well the uncertainty which ensued—the dreadful suspicion of owls and hawks and disaster, and the resolute hope that Nature had at last asserted itself. Tweet was banded, however, and might still be heard from again near her old home.

Mr. Chips, who always sends us a Christmas card with his portrait on it from Pennsylvania, is a yellow-billed cuckoo, rather rare for his locality. Each spring we receive from him quantities of yellow daffodils in perfect condition, and a note thoughtfully supplying the information that they have not been sprayed with any insecticide, and so are safe for Che-Wee to nibble, which he does. Mr. Chips has trouble with his tail feathers—can't seem to keep them—but otherwise enjoys himself hugely and when taken outdoors refuses to depart. He regards his cage as his castle, and goes into it and turns his back whenever he gets bored, a privilege which is enviable on many counts from the human point of view. He sits on his lady's finger and listens to the Philharmonic for a solid hour at a time—and worse, he read *Kissing Kin* over her shoulder, page by page.

Butch is a purple finch *californicus,* who also sings and also doesn't achieve full male plumage. Harry James's trumpet is said always to tune him up. (Che-Wee prefers Hawaiian music to sing to—the Mitchell-Waikiki influence, I presume.) Butch is afraid of branches, but he lives with and dominates *eight cats,* and shares their cat-nip. This I would like to see.

An albino grackle, very handsome by his photograph; a starling who is learning to whistle *God Save the King;* a turtle dove who hates to go to bed just like people, and anyway tries to sleep on the master's pillow; an undersized hermit thrush with a permanently damaged wing who sings ecstatically to classical music on the radio and eats from the dog's dish alongside its owner; a sparrow who is seven and a half and quarrelsome, but always flies back in from outdoors; all these and many others have written to Che-Wee more than once, and we are always delighted to hear about their adventures and accomplishments. And if sometimes the ornithologist in the house indulges in a somewhat old-fashioned look at some of the stories—such as the white-crowned sparrow who lies down on its back in a little bed and is covered with a handky, but there is a picture of him doing it—Che-Wee and I are endlessly agog at what our mail may contain, and we believe it all. Because we know, between us, that there are a lot of things mere scientists never discover, that they are a tribe that like Skippy's little friend are always belittlin', and that any bird with ordinary advantages does things every day that are not in the observations of the most broadminded behaviorist.

A gratifying aspect of our correspondence is that so many people ask for More, and inquire about Che-Wee's present health, and suggest a further report on his doings. And so, along with how I turned into a farmer, I am setting down here what I have learned from him since his book was written, and how he finds himself today, thank-you-very-much, he would like to say. It is written, as before, with his daily supervision and assistance.

This swift, generous response in an uneasy, driven world to the courage and the humor contained in one little ounce of feathered life—he could be mailed anywhere with a three-cent stamp stuck on his tail—has made me think more than twice.

When I was a small child I was fond of a story by Marion Hill about boy and girl twins named Rex and Regina and their very high-collared mother—I can still see the illustrations—who believed in modern child-psychology methods when such ideas were much more novel than they seem now. As part of the twins' education and training, they were required to care for a particularly noisy canary, turn about, to teach them responsibility and consideration for all God's creatures. And young Regina, bored with feeding it and cleaning its cage, was wont to remark resignedly, "Come along, you God-screecher, you," when it was her turn for responsibility and consideration. This is the first joke I can remember appreciating, and it never grew stale.

New York isn't much of a place for pets, and I have spent most of my life there, or travelling, so I was not well acquainted with God's creatures myself when Che-Wee was wished on to me a few years ago. But before long I heard myself saying that if ever we lost Che-Wee—we like to pretend that such a possibility is extremely remote—I should at once get another bird, even if I had to buy a mere canary out of a shop, to fill up in the smallest degree the void his absence from our lives would create. I would never have the nerve to take a wild bird like Che-Wee that was not in distress, or that had visible parents to support it. If it died, or even if it didn't, I couldn't forgive myself for depriving it of the possible fun it might have had living a normal bird's life outdoors. With Che-Wee we had no choice. He was lost and deserted. We took him in or else. But any bird, I heard myself saying, even one out of a shop, would have some character of its own, which would expand under family life, and it would develop, not into another Che-Wee, not even into something just as good, but into Something, period.

From time to time I go into pet shops to buy seeds and knick-knacks for Che-Wee. There is always a row of cages, each inhabited by a bird, usually a canary, and I began to catch myself eyeing them questioningly. Every so often a personality would emerge; a pale blonde canary with jade green wing quills, minding its own business at its seed cup in Macy's basement; a brownish canary with a yellow breast and cap, showing off its song fit to bust at Gimbel's; an oyster grey and white "Yorkshire imported," singing with modest sweetness, price-tagged $27.50; a cinnamon bird, with a white breast, who said "Hi!" when I looked at it. . . . And then last spring I saw the Hungarian Finch.

He was an expensive bird to begin with, in much too small a cage, for he was a size larger than a canary, with a long white tail which had got rather bedraggled. But the worst of it was, the Hungarian Finch saw me. I had moved in close to the row of cages behind the counter while I was waiting for the clerk, and was looking over the collection of some two dozen birds, and wondering idly what Che-Wee would do if I brought home a friend for him some day. Was he ever lonesome for his own feathered kind? Would he be jealous? Would he bully a canary, or be bullied by it? And then the Finch and I caught each other's eye.

He was yellow and white, this outsize canary, and compared to Che-Wee, his eyes were too small for his face. But he came over to the side of the cage and put one pink foot up on the bars and poked his head through and gazed at me winningly. It was embarrassing, the way the stare of a baby in a bus can be, because in the circumstances it is difficult either to make friends or to ignore it. I moved away. In a few minutes I drifted back, and it happened again. It happened four times, and by then I was ready to buy the thing, *and* a good-sized cage, and hang the expense.

Only one consideration held me back. We were leaving for the country house in a few days, and every minute till then was full, and after I got there I had to finish a book script against a June deadline. There simply wasn't time to introduce this little stranger into Che-Wee's life and observe the effect and deal with any situation which arose. If I took the new bird with us to the country and then Che-Wee hated it—or worse, if the new bird, being bigger, tried to boss Che-Wee around in his own house—I would be stuck with it. And carrying *two* bird-cages to Vermont, even in a Pullman. . . .

I bought Che-Wee's seed, which was what I had come for, and walked out, without looking back, and I have regretted it up and down ever since. Weeks later, when I was again in New York, I went back to the shop, and of course the Hungarian Finch was gone. If it was you who bought him, or you, or you, please let me know how he is doing, because I shall never be able to forget him as long as I live.

I now found myself with a Message: *Everybody ought to have a bird.*

In particular, every invalid, every inactive older person,

everyone who lives alone, male or female, as well as every child, should own and be owned by a bird. People who have been left lonely by a death or a wedding should have one. Unlike a dog or a cat, it's no trouble to feed and clean up after, and it is a much more welcome visitor to your week-end hostess. It doesn't have to go out for a walk in bad weather, it travels easily in a small covered cage in trains or cars, its food comes prepared in a tidy box, and if you're really busy ten minutes a day will do for its chores. If you want to take more trouble, if you need something to do and something to care for, the opportunity is endless. You can begin by filling a large baking-pan with earth and making him a garden—a hunk of turf, a big stone, a tiny tree, a glass dish sunk to ground level for a pool, a bare patch of earth to sow bird-seed in for him to mow down himself as the green shoots come up, a little sand-pile for grit—he will be touchingly grateful if you either set the open-bottomed cage over the pan now and then or let him come out of the cage and play in it. Don't be afraid he won't go back in the cage, if his food is there. To a canary, the cage is home and not confinement. He feels secure in it.

But you must always take precautions about open windows and closing doors when he is out of the cage. Windows must be screened, for a cage-bird that gets out "free" in a northern climate is not likely to survive long. And a bird will always light on the top of a door, confident that the door cannot be closed while he is there. Don't let your bird out of the cage till he has been with you a week, and feels at home in your rooms. Don't expect him to sing, either, until the strangeness has worn off. Have patience. Talk to him and feed him tid-bits. It may take some time for him to settle down after he leaves the shop.

Birds are husky little things, if kept clean and warm and wisely fed. A draught is the worst danger. The cage mustn't stand between open door and open window, and it shouldn't be left long in full sunlight, as it gets very hot. It should always be covered with a dark cloth at night, both for safety from draughts and for darkness. And get him as large a cage as you can afford. The perches have to be taken out and scraped *each day*, to make sure the bird doesn't start having sore feet, which can be fatal. Bird men always recommend the substitution of at least one smaller perch than the ones that come with the cages, so that the bird must close its feet and grip. Wooden knitting needles can be cut and slit at the ends to fit, or a small twig can be inserted. The paper in the bottom of the cage must be changed every morning too, and covered with fresh gravel—bird-gravel out of a package, because ordinary sand may have goodness knows what in it of sharp particles and foreign matter which might cause trouble inside—wild birds know enough to choose, presumably. You can buy paper with a coating of sand already on it, which is absorbent and cleaner, but loose bird-gravel should still be sprinkled on top of that. *Never* use the sandpaper sheaths sold for perches, though—very hard on the feet. The only way to keep its claws short enough is to trim them every few months with a pinch cutter. No bird likes this, as it means being caught in the hand, and I hate it myself, but people in bird shops make nothing of it, and unless you cut too close it doesn't hurt. Only the tip, beyond the end of the vein, should be snipped off.

A piece of cuttle-bone fastened to the inside of the bars is as much of a necessity as his seed-cup, which must be refilled every morning with fresh seed stirred into what he has left the day before. Every now and then turn it out into a big dish and blow the husks out, or throw it away and give him a whole new deal. He ought not to have salty or greasy food, and not much sweet beyond a crumb of sponge cake. Celery leaves and the tender tops of the stalk are better for him than lettuce, of which he should have only the green outer edges, and wedges of orange and apple are popular as daily treats. The seed plumes of bluegrass from the edge of the lawn is welcome. Fasten his greens to the bars at the end of the perch with a pinch clothespin, so that it doesn't get down in the bottom where he can wool it around in the dirt. And don't leave fruit or greens there all day for him to nibble at or they will finally upset him. An hour or so is enough, then take it away.

Now, don't just walk into the first shop you come to and say I'll take that one, and hand over the money. Hang around, look 'em over, take your time, give him a chance. Somewhere in the row of cages there may be one bird that belongs specially to you—like my Hungarian Finch. There are a few simple rules about buying a bird, of course. Don't adopt a mopey one with uneven, uncared-for feathers just because you're sorry for him as I have been tempted to do. If he's that way in the shop he may die very soon. Be sure his feet are smooth and healthy without sores or knobs. Notice if he has kept his fanny clean, a sure sign of a bird's condition. The chances are you don't want a nervous bird, any more than a mopey one, and some canaries do jitter. Take one that eats and chirps and moves normally while you watch—not one that hops perpetually from perch to perch and tries to get through the bars— he will be harder to tame. Ask for a young bird—you will keep him longer. If you think singing will tire or bore you, get a female. They're cheaper, too, and often get tamer.

I'm not just talking through my hat, because during the past year I *have* bought canaries, and Che-Wee *doesn't* care for them, but I do, and I know now what I long suspected—that a bird is worth whatever you pay for it, whether it's $2.50 at Woolworth's or $25 at a fancy shop. None of them will be Che-Wee, of course—he, like Gable, is the King. But if you once own one, you're done for. An inexpensive canary in an inexpensive cage is more money's worth of companionship, beauty, and spontaneous laughter than most purchases many times the size in a dreary world. After a few weeks you wouldn't trade him for a diamond necklace.

He will learn to take food from your fingers, he will learn to sit on your finger to eat—the vitality and confidence in the grip of a bird's feet on your finger must be experienced to be believed. He will be feeding quietly in his cage and then catch sight of you as you appear in the doorway and greet you with an inquiring chirp of recognition and joy that breaks you all up. He always wants company. Most of us do.

There are, I know, cautious people who are afraid to have pets because they dread the inevitable grief when the short life span comes to an end. This seems to me nonsense, and cowardly besides. Your dog dies, yes, or your canary—canaries live to be eighteen years old, incidentally. But then it dies. Don't think I don't expect to shed tears some day myself. But it's not your mother or your husband, you can buy another, and even in spite of you before long the new personality, the new tricks, and above all the confiding, flattering trust of the little creature will make its own place in your life. You will not forget the lost one. But while you cannot buy for cold cash any human friendship worth the name, you *can* buy for a very small sum the devoted companionship of a pet who is in need of someone to love.

Almost everybody has days when they wake up feeling as though nothing is much of any good. But by the time a bird has been wakened and fed and cleaned and has begun his own day with his usual gay confidence in everybody's good intentions, you find you're feeling a little better yourself. I don't get a commission on canary sales, believe it or not, and I am not by nature a do-gooder. But people might as well have fun, if there is any such thing these days. And if you haven't got a bird you're missing a lot of fun.

In pursuit of my conviction that a bird can help enormously in the long adjustment to living alone after a bereavement, I arranged to have a well-born canary brought up to me from New York by a guest who was arriving opportunely, so that I could give it to Elmer's mother. I wanted a singer, as I thought that would be cheerful for her. So Petey arrived, a long-legged, bouncy young male bird with an exquisite soft voice. He was to stay with us for a few days till he got over the excitement of the journey and learned to come out of his cage and play around—then he was to go on to his new home. I would also have an opportunity during his visit to observe Che-Wee's reactions to another bird in the house, and decide if I wanted to add to my responsibilities in that direction.

I found it very little trouble to valet Petey and keep him clean and fed. First thing in the morning he got fresh seed and water in his cups and the bottom of the cage was removed to be cleaned and he was set over his bath dish. If after a decent interval he hadn't bathed, I skipped it, and the fresh bottom was replaced and the cage carried out on to Che-Wee's screen porch, which always caused Petey to yip with joy and burst into song. It also often caused Che-Wee to retire haughtily into the house, for so far from giving any evidence of pleasure at feathered company, he regarded Petey with a sort of tolerant contempt. Later when I encouraged Petey to come out of the cage he would romp up to Che-Wee on the same branch, full of friendliness and charm, and Che-Wee would open his beak threateningly and chitter at him. Petey was always nonplussed, but bore no malice. His singing left Che-Wee unimpressed, and no duets occurred. When Petey tuned up, Che-Wee withdrew into his dignity, which has always been immense.

As the time approached for Petey to move on, I thought seriously of sending for one of his brothers some time soon, in the hope that Che-Wee wouldn't mind too much and might even learn to fraternize. And then one night a field-mouse got into Petey's cage and killed him.

It was one of the beastliest little tragedies I have ever come up against, and I blamed myself endlessly and still do. I brought him there and let it happen to him. So much joy and youngness, extinguished in terror and black despair, with no one hearing, no one to the rescue. The cage was the trouble, I think, as it was not a new model—it was a pretty round one, but its unusual shape meant that at the top the crosswise wires were far apart and made it possible for the murderer to squeeze through. The cage was sitting where Che-Wee's stouter and heavier sleeping-cage had sat many a night before—on the dresser in the downstairs bedroom. The seed-cup in Petey's cage, which was never in Che-Wee's as he only slept there, acted as bait, of course. When I took the cloth off that morning, expecting the excited chirp with which Petey always greeted a new day, he was on the bottom of the cage, all chewed. You could see where the wires had been forced apart. I was very sick indeed.

The same thing could have happened to Che-Wee long ago, and although I subconsciously agreed with everybody who was tactlessly relieved that it was *not* Che-Wee, I resented on poor Petey's behalf the implication that he was more easily spared. And for days I was beset in my imagination by the hopeless fluttering in the darkness and the sharp teeth of the

Thing he could not even see. We took new precautions now for Che-Wee's safety, hung his sleeping-cage from a hook in the ceiling, set mouse-traps every night which had to be sprung every morning before he was let out. But it was all too late for Petey, and I was a long time accepting that.

I didn't feel that I deserved another canary, ever. Then I began to see it a different way. I owed something to Petey, still. I owed him all the love and safety I could find for other canaries. He had missed his little destiny, which was to bring laughter and delight to an aging, lonely woman. But another bird could do it for him, and have a wonderful life himself. Another bird is doing it now. And by some freak of coincidence, when his lady came to name him, although he had been to her a complete surprise and she knew nothing about his predecessor, she called him—Pete.

16.

OF COURSE IT'S NOT really a farm, because it hasn't got livestock. Last spring I dreamed briefly of a baby Angus bull, which Elmer had a chance to buy, for beef. He would have looked very nice, grazing in the middle distance behind the charged wire which separates the small hayfield from the vegetable garden. That field could easily be fenced to include a bit of the brook for water, and it needs manure fertilizer. . . . But not with The Barn on, there wasn't time for both.

Garbage is difficult to dispose of, and more than once I have spoken wistfully of a pig. With a small movable pen there is no need for it to disfigure the landscape. Eggs were short even in the country that summer, and I wished we had hens. You can hear horrific stories of the price of feed and other complications which end by causing each hen to cost twice as much as if you bought it dressed for the table, and all its possible eggs besides. But I know two women who don't *look* as though they had any more sense than I have, but they have both made an excellent thing out of chickens and preserved their manicures and their social calenders intact. With Elmer to help me, surely even I could manage to come out ahead on a few chickens, and still get the new book done on time. . . .

Elmer, like Barkis, is always willing. There is no question of my having to say tactfully to the one person whose daily chores would be considerably added to, "*Would* you mind—?" The necessary repairs and additions and seasonal routine of the place are still quite enough for one man single-handed, but Elmer is all for raising things. So we did get as far as bees.

I never knew much about bees, but there is a good deal of talk about a shortage of pollinating insects, especially since the reckless post-war use of new DDT solutions began. Elmer has a friend who for years has done quite well setting out bee-hives in people's orchards on a business arrangement, but just as we were about to conclude a deal with him for a couple of hives the bee-man lost forty-four hives in an orchard which had just been sprayed. Nobody thought to tell him about it before he brought his bees in, and they not only died in their thousands, but the hives and equipment had all to be destroyed. There appeared to be no redress. He could only start out philosophically again to build up his stock with new queens and new hives.

If this happened once, and was accepted as a not unheard-of occurrence among bee-men, it must happen again and again. The loss is not only in dollars and bee mortality, but in pollinization, and hence in the yield of orchards, gardens, and fields. But people continue to buy almost any advertised insecticide and use it nearsightedly against some specific insect pest of their own, without contemplating the incidental damage to other insects which are innocent, and to the birds who feed on them and die of poisoning in their turn.

The subject of insecticides is not one to be mastered in a few hours study, as I realized after consulting Brayton Eddy at the New York Zoological Park—but it is apparent from the briefest survey that the indiscriminate amateur use of sprays, continually disrupting the natural balance of life which has been painfully arrived at down the centuries, can prove more deadly to the human race than the atom bomb. Insect pests appear to be alarmingly on the increase—partly because of new opportunities to arrive from foreign parts as stowaways, leaving their natural biological enemies behind, and partly from our much discussed injudicious planting operations. But the one thing we should not do is to rush round drenching everything with any and every spray on the market. An insect-less world would soon shrivel up and starve to death.

Disappointed of our ready-made bees, I then discovered that you could buy bees from the mail-order house, complete with fertilized queen and drones, and accompanied by all their toiletries, and I began to look into that. "Three-banded certified Italian queens, guaranteed disease-proof and purely mated, $1.45 each. Three-pound package of bees, best honey-making strain, fine pollinators, with a state health certificate, $5.45. Shipped in combless packages from apiaries in Georgia, express collect. State date bees are wanted." So many *pounds* of bees, like butter or beans. But would they like Vermont? Well, we could try.

The hives, at $5.90 each, were shipped knocked down in

pieces and had to be put together and painted before the bees came. There were a lot of extra parts not included in the price of the hive—an old mail-order custom—such as brood foundations, supers, queen excluders, honey-boxes, bee-gloves, face-veil, smoker, hive-tool, etc. It comes to about $30 to set up a hive of bees for business. Again, the initial cost. After that, just the small expenditure for new bees when needed. If the swarm was established and sturdy when cold weather came they could be wintered underneath the barn, and start the next season with no additional expense whatever.

We sent for the hive and the and-so-forths and promptly received a large weighty carton. It was a chilly rainy day when it came, and Elmer opened it on the woodshed floor with all the pleased anticipation of a kid with a new meccano set. That's about what it was, too. I never saw so many pieces to anything. Lovely new white wood, cut into what looked like millions of small notched strips and slabs, accompanied by little bags of nails and metal fitments, and a large pink Instruction Sheet, which as usual had been written by someone who knew so well what he was talking about that he couldn't express himself clearly.

That beehive was the only time I have ever seen Elmer flummoxed by something which had to be put together or taken apart, but for a little while it really had him going. Starr Cooper arrived with the milk and sat down on the woodpile and put in his two cents' worth every now and then just for fun. Elmer was never anything but good-natured when we laughed and guyed him for incompetence. But it took most of the afternoon, and the only way he finally got it together was by ignoring the Instruction Sheet and using his own judgment, fitting in piece by enigmatic piece, and even then it looked as though he might have a few left over. Eventually it was ready for its coat of white paint, and then we waited for the bees.

They arrived, singing, in a wire cage the size of two big books laid end to end. They were in a V-shaped cluster over the tin can suspended in the middle which allowed syrup to seep out from tiny holes to sustain them on the journey. Those around the outer edge were hungrier than the ones next the can, and consequently crosser, and the can was empty. There were a few dead ones in the bottom. The queen was in a little box inside the cage, sealed up in candy with several drones. The bees would eat the candy away and liberate her and kill the drones, when given the chance.

The newly painted hive was dry and in its place in the lee of the cherry hedge in the little hayfield below the wire. According to directions on the bee-cage, we made a syrup with sugar, equal parts, and put it in a quart jar upended in a saucer with a nail laid between to make a slow seepage—like a water-dish for chickens—and set it in the hive with a few foundations in frames. Elmer donned the veil and the elbow length bee-gloves—very professional, and very necessary—stoked up the smoker with excelsior, just in case, pried the cage open and set it inside the hive, took out the queen's box and made it available, put the lid gently on the hive and came away without getting stung. We had to wait five days before we could peek, for they mustn't be disturbed till they had settled down a bit, and then they could have more syrup.

At the end of that time the cage was empty except for the dead ones on its floor, and the syrup was all gone from the jar. The queen was out, the drones were dead, the sentries were set, and the workers were busily going in and out. We took out the cage, gave them another jar of syrup, and waited five more days. Then we took the empty jar away. The first wax cells were growing fast on the foundations, a miracle of symmetry and design.

So that's all there is to starting bees. They arrived so late in the season that we let them keep their first honey, and expected to give them extra syrup for the winter if they needed it. They seemed to thrive, and we sent off at once for one more hive and established it in the back field on the other side of the cherry hedge. The two white-painted hives look very nice, and the golden bees are easily distinguishable from the larger, darker local variety as they work the garden flowers side by side. If it hadn't been for The Barn, Elmer would have made a bee-box and brought in a wild swarm too, but there was no time.

Once it stopped raining—which was not until after the fruit blossom had gone, so the apple crop was ruined—it turned into a glorious hot summer, running just as everyone had gloomily prophesied in May into a bad drought. And once the work on The Barn really began to progress it was possible for me, at least, to relax a bit and concentrate, perhaps a little reluctantly, on the unfinished book.

I have never sympathized much with the If-I-had-a-rose-covered-cottage-in-the-country-I-could-be-a-genius frame of mind. It doesn't pay to sit around and wait for that. Most of us do better to settle for being a carthorse right where we are. Somerset Maugham tells about the man who for twenty years amused himself with thinking what he would write when he really got down to it, and for another twenty with what he would have written if the fates had been kinder. Not long ago I read a book by Robert van Gelder, who spent a lot of time and I imagine a great deal of tact gathering the opinions of a list of well-known writers on writing, and published the result. And since then I have got quite fascinated reading about writers. I have rather gone in for it—Maugham's *The Summing Up*, Vera Brittain's *On Being an Author*, Kenneth Roberts' *I Wanted to Write*, Edna Ferber, Katherine Brush, Paul Gallico, Mary Roberts Rinehart, Edith Wharton, G. B. Stern, Willa Cather, and, with particular joy, Sir Osbert Sitwell's delightfully Gothic memoirs written in his wonderful Gothic prose—and I note with respect and a twinge of envy the minimum requirements set forth by the experts for writing a book. It's not really an easy job, although, as has been frequently pointed out, you can sit down to do it, and although one of the best recommendations for its accomplishment is Sinclair Lewis's terse remark about the application of the seat of the pants to the seat of the chair. According to the general rules it seems quite impossible for me to have written a book at all since I left England in the autumn of 1939. Whereas the count is actually seven.

One of the things a writer of books is asked oftenest by non-writers is "*How* do you write—when?—where?—with what?—" etc., etc. And I have come to the conclusion that they must really want to know, instead of just making conversation. So—I write the first draught in longhand with a pencil, because that is quickest for scratching out, in lined notebooks from Woolworth's. And because I use a sort of shorthand longhand, with my own arbitrary abbreviations for certain standard recurrent words, it is all unreadable except to me. Then I type it myself, with one carbon, double-spaced, and by the time I have read it through once many pages are so interlined that they are again undecipherable to any eye but mine—rewritten, as Ilka Chase put it in *Free Admission*, till they look "like the scrawlings of an hysterical octopus"— and have to be typed again. And so on, ad infinitum.

When the final manuscript is sent to the publisher it is, I am told, unusually tidy, but I could not myself tell how it sounded if it were not. Nevertheless, no one ever types it but me, some pages over and over again and then once more, just to clean it up for the printer. My research—and most books require some sort of research, even if the setting is modern—is written in pencil notes in smaller notebooks from Woolworth's, and runs to hundreds of these pages as I have no memory worth speaking of, and must write everything down, under headings and in careful chronology. Often a whole day's reading at the desk or in the library yields not one visible result to be found in the book itself. Often many days of correspondence and effort go into collecting material which at most covers a page or so in the book—as in the case of the St. Dunstan's work in *Kissing Kin*. For some obscure, dogged reason I consider this worth while and I take satisfaction in it. It is quite beyond me to filter information on any subject second-hand through a secretary or reader, or to filter my own ideas through a typist to the printer. I must do it all myself, obstinately, lovingly, toilsomely, in my own muddling way, though by now I have through trial and error evolved what is—to me at least—a system of sorts. Obviously, since no one can help me at all, I am best left alone to wrestle it out.

I mentioned a library, and this is a subject on which I feel competent and obliged to enlarge. After months of work each summer in the Reading-room of the British Museum, I was thoroughly spoilt for any other surroundings when I returned to New York in the autumn. During the winters I made abortive attempts to find a comparable atmosphere, and my experience always ended in blood-pressure and hard feelings. The Morgan Library was the exception, and Miss Greene gave me the warmest welcome there, but its usefulness was limited by the nature of the work I was doing. The management of the library at Forty-second Street and Fifth Avenue has changed since the last time I set foot there some years ago, and so my opinion of it is obviously dated and is now often heatedly challenged. But the procedure I encountered there used to suggest a Freshman entry into Sing Sing rather than something labelled a Free Public Library. No doubt all the precautions and regulations and restrictions, which seemed to stop just short of fingerprinting and which were then imposed upon the prospective reader by people who suffered from a general dearth of charm, were necessary in an institution given to the use of a very mixed public notoriously careless of its privileges and prone to take advantage, and the loss and wilful damage to library property were said still to be considerable. But the notoriously law-abiding British have another system.

There is no charge for a membership card admitting you to the Reading-room in Bloomsbury. Your introduction must come from another reader in good standing, or from someone known to be a responsible citizen of London. Once that little white card is secured you're on your own. You may carry a capacious attaché bag in and out each day, containing your own books and notebooks which you wish to use in conjunction with the volumes drawn from the Museum shelves. There is no inspection at the glass doors marked Readers Only, which open off the main entrance hall, and within a remarkably few days the two uniformed men on duty there know you by sight and greet you with an easy gesture of welcome so that there is no need even to show your card.

There used to be life tickets, but these are now extinct—the word is the Museum's choice—and the longest duration is six months. Still, I have never heard of anyone having formally to renew a ticket which has run its six months span. Anyone can get a day ticket by applying at the Director's office and giving a good reason. It will admit you only once behind the glass doors, and the sample I have in my collection says it is for "research procedure." There are seven kinds of tickets—the Newspaper Library, Manuscript Room, Oriental Books and Print Room all require separate cards. In the Manuscript Room they bring you priceless things loose in drawers. Your fingers rest where royal fingers long gone to dust once rested as they wrote, with no glass case between. A specimen page from the diary of Edward VI was on display in a glass case, but during the work on *The Tudor Wench* I held the rest of it in my hands, mounted in a big album, and turned through it at will to copy from it. Edward died in 1553 at the age of fifteen. The paper they gave him to write on is like a cheap pencil pad of the present time, greyish and coarse. His handwriting, unlike that of his sisters, is sloping and strangely modern.

In the big circular Reading-room, lined with accessible shelves in three tiers above and below iron galleries, you work at a vast padded black leather desk with ample elbow room which cannot be encroached upon. The desk is one of a long, continuous row radiating from the Superintendent's circular central desk and the catalogue shelves like the spoke of a wheel. It has a solid front which rises high enough to conceal the person seated facing you along the other side of the spoke. It is provided with a built-in book-shelf, a folding book-rest, pen, inkwell (full), pen-wiper, paper-cutter, and blotting pad. It has a hatpeg and a footstool underneath, and an individual hanging lamp with a stiff maroon shade above, besides the adequate central lighting. It is also equipped with a ventilating system which to an American is only a private, built-in draft, but the British thrive on drafts. In spite of them, there is the pungent, unmistakable Reading-room atmosphere, out of which occasionally emerge one or two identifiable whiffs like well-thumbed book-leaves or damp wool or latent pipe smoke, but mostly it is just a permanent, amorphous, all-over, not unpleasant Smell, which I am sure I could recognize blindfold in Timbuctoo a hundred years from now.

The catalogue, which praise be to God is *not* card-indexed, is contained in mammoth black leather scrap-books in the shelves which form the curved outer edge of the hub of the wheel. It is made up of printed items pasted to the pages, with room left for additions. New, freshly pasted-up, alternative pages were constantly interchanged and added. The man who sits at the center of the hub is unhurried, patient, helpful, even fatherly. You can ask him *anything*, and he always knows, with a smile.

After consulting the catalogue and making out your request slip with your seat number on it—you can take any vacant seat, though habitués have their favorites, year in and year out, and custom reserves some of these even if they are not occupied at the beginning of the day—you drop your slip in a box on the central desk and return to your chair. In no time at all a rubber-tired cart arrives at your side and a smiling boy lays your books on the desk before you, says "Cue," which is the British shorthand for Thank-you and is usually spoken by the person rendering the service as well as the receiver, and goes away—and the world is yours. There was no known limit to the number of books you could command at one time when I was there, and some of the oldsters sat amongst towers of them higher than the grizzled head of the reader. War time staff shortage has now imposed a limit, I am told, but I doubt if that lasts. One of the few restrictions placed on the reader's choice reads: *Recent fiction is not issued except for special purposes.* I have no idea what the Museum considers Special Purposes, but I do know that Recent Fiction means anything published within the last five years!

When you go out to lunch or tea, or morning elevenses, you leave everything just as it is. The desk is yours as long as any possession of yours, such as a folded newspaper or a notebook, lies upon it, and will remain undisturbed. I was always convinced that my purse as well could lie there alone in perfect safety. When you are ready to go home you return your books to the central desk and receive back your request slips, which cancels your responsibility. If you will want them again you carry them to a different wicket in the hub under a sign which says *Kept Books*, write out duplicate slips for them, and they will await you there with your markers in them for two clear days. It is not considered funny to consider the sign funny. It means what it says.

Further, there is an inner sanctum known as the North Library, where the Museum's blessings flow even freer. Because my sponsor there was a dyed-in-the-wool reader and an authority on the Tudor period, I was privileged to ring the bell at the little glass door behind the Superintendent's desk. Some cheerful book-boy would open the locked door from within and I passed through the stacks and into the large room beyond, where I owned for the period of my stay each summer a table in one of the side bays. The point about this was that unless you were working with case books—that is, valuable editions of early chronicles or special bindings or association volumes which were locked up at night—you never turned anything in until you had finished with it, and your same copies stayed there on your table with your markers in them, day after day. On rare occasions you received a slip saying that the book was being asked for by another reader, and that meant that in common decency you must release it, as you knew by experience that *he* had already received a slip, perhaps more than once, saying that the book was in use by another reader. The Superintendent of the North Library was even more fatherly than the one in the round room, and the legend was that he had started as a book-boy in his teens, which was the sort of promotion it used to be for a ranker in the Army to achieve a glittering commission, and I hope it was true, for it was nothing but a credit to him.

There were many good stories about the eccentricities of the habitual readers of both sexes, some of whom looked older than God and had spent their lives in a blissful dream of scholarship in the Isaac Disraeli tradition. The one I liked best was about the absent-minded he-ancient who rose at the end of the day, picked up the chair in which he had been sitting—they are very heavy, with padded black leather seats—inverted it over his head with the seat resting on his hat and the legs in the air, and started for the door. Before he had gone many steps an unflustered attendant touched him on the arm and said quietly, "We always leave the chairs here, sir." "Ah, yes —quite so," agreed the old gentleman, surrendering the Museum's property with no fuss at all.

Forgive this excursion into nostalgia. All of it may be altered beyond recognition by this latest war, and that is one of the things I shall learn when at last I return to England full of hope and apprehension. Much of what I loved so much has suffered or vanished forever. But I doubt if the British Museum, which has seen a good many wars since it was merely Montagu House, will prove very receptive to change or alleged improvements.

Its nearest equivalent in New York is the Society Library

in East 79th Street, where it is true you pay a modest sum each year to enjoy a leisurely atmosphere and perfect librarianship, and which in comparison is of course very small—though in my experience they can produce practically anything you can possibly require. There too you may leave material on the desk overnight if you must, as I have done with the tremendous bound volumes of *The Queen* and other periodicals which were necessary to the background of the Williamsburg books. I discovered the place belatedly, but now I could not function without it. It is only a year younger than the British Museum, having been founded in 1754 during the first year of the French and Indian war, and its early ledgers carry the names of the fathers of our country, as it was once housed in the same building as the First Continental Congress and the delegates all had membership privileges. It has moved several times since then, and its present quarters provide all the comforts of home, including ashtrays and armchairs in the members' reading-room. There is also accommodation for non-members in the big catalogue room on the ground floor, where general reference books and the library card catalogue are available to anyone who wishes to consult them. I consider this a very long-headed arrangement, as even casual readers must often be seduced by their reception and surroundings into paying the membership fee ($18 yearly) in order to enjoy the further benefits, such as unrestricted mail service and the privilege of purchasing slightly used copies as they are culled, and private work-rooms on the top floor where you can use your typewriter or consult with a collaborator. My beloved friend, Marion King, who came there fresh from her librarians' school some years ago, can remember when the trustees exercised a fatherly censorship over the readers' choice of books—so that twelve brand new copies of *Three*

Weeks languished untouched on the shelves until the demand for it ceased, because someone had protested that it was not quite the sort of thing to be circulated. One copy is available there today, if anyone wants it, but the benevolent tyranny which suppressed it in its flagrant youth no longer exists.

As I read the written testimony of other writers, the first gulf I noticed between myself and my professional betters was an almost universal reluctance to begin the day's work—such as in Edna Ferber's moving description of her many subterfuges for delay, from reading the newspaper through to the back pages which meant nothing whatever to her, to picking up threads off the carpet. Vera Brittain mentions the stern self-discipline she requires to refrain from answering letters or doing accounts, in order to postpone the fatal necessity for creative thought. But foolish me, when I see a chance to get in a few hours work there is no fashionable inclination to dawdle.

"Writing," writes Vera Brittain, for whose work as a novelist I have much respect although I cannot agree with her fundamental pacifist viewpoint, "Writing, unlike some other forms of art, is essentially a solitary job. It demands, over long periods of time, an exacting life which must inevitably appear egotistical and even anti-social to those who find their natural expression in community living and group-thinking. His need for prolonged solitude is something of which a writer finds it extremely hard to convince anyone but his fellow-authors. When he insists that he requires it, his relatives are skeptical and his friends are amused. Even his admiring public tends at times to feel that his emphasis on the importance of quiet concentration can be taken with a grain of salt. . . ."

Consider also Sir Osbert Sitwell's noble-edifice-of-days passage which it is wicked to tear from its context in *Laughter in the Next Room*, but which I cannot quote here in full: "—nevertheless to have the energy and leisure in which to give the process of creation and growth its chance of fullest development, the author must be allowed to dwell within a nobly proportioned edifice of days and hours, which offers vistas of space on every side so that he does not have to hurry or cramp his productions. He cannot press out the final flicker of fire or obtain the last spark of energy, if he knows he must soon begin preparations to leave his work in a fortnight's time, in order to deliver a lecture, or, it may be, to see his mother. He must be granted, if he is to achieve his best, as many days as are necessary for him not to be obliged to count them, a period peaceful and unharassed. Adventures, troubles, joys, the iruption, even, of a dearest friend into the quiet and regular rhythm of life that a writer has to establish, can break up a whole book. Moreover, if employed upon a poem or something which requires an equivalent trancelike intensity, the writer will remain for some days, or it may be weeks, in so nervous and supersensitive a state, or feel so dull and numb to the outer world, that any slight shock, a pointless altercation, or a mere change in his mode of existence, may destroy the life in what he is at work creating."

That is really authorship de luxe—*as many days as are necessary for him not to be obliged to count them.* . . . Even in those old days before what we now call the War, having demoted the 1914-'18 affair to being called the Last War, which it was anything but—even back in the spacious Thirties when for weeks at a time, alone in London, I kept my own fantastic hours and did *not* keep any sort of social calendar, and often never spoke all day to anyone but a waiter and a bookboy in the Museum Reading-room, even then there was always the deadline of a sailing date looming over me, so that anything I hadn't got into my notebooks by then had to wait till next year, unless I could find a copy of some particular book in Charing Cross Road and could afford to buy it and bring it home with me. (Sir Osbert's magnificently involute style is beginning to affect my own.)

Then Hitler got loose and I couldn't go to England any more. I worked at home the year round, I was ill, I got better, I sold a little house in Maine and bought a bigger one in Vermont, I got quite well again, with only a tendency to give out suddenly if I go back to working later and later at night because the world is quiet then. . . . "Some day," says Mary Roberts Rinehart in her autobiography, "someone will write a book about that frantic search of the creative worker for silence and freedom, not only from interruption but from the fear of interruption." . . .

The nearest I ever came, or ever will come, so far as I can see, to the rose-covered cottage for genius, was in Buckinghamshire as mentioned heretofore. But even then I was far from the trancelike condition acknowledged by Sir Osbert. The main difference between what there is to do in the country and in the city is that in the country it is more fun, you have a greater choice of diversion, and the telephone doesn't ring so often because it costs people more to call you. In Bucks my rented roses developed greenfly, and I nursed them with sprays and took neighborly advice. And the faded flowers in the border had all to be kept cut off so things would go on blooming for the owners' return. And there was a new stove to be experimented with and new recipes the tapioca pudding was not a success. And you could have tea on the lawn in bright-colored deckchairs, which took longer to prepare and then you lingered over it in the afternoon sun. The half-mile walk to the village for provisions—I had no maid beyond the chauffeur's wife up at the Big House, who came in to "do for me" every morning—that walk always spun itself out into conversations with people met coming and going or in the shops, and was likely to end in strolls in the wrong direction from the typewriter. To return to Maugham, as every writer must, he blocked out a window facing the desk in his work-room because the view of the blue Mediterranean distracted his mind.

Perhaps I lack character for so Spartan a resolution, or per-haps I just don't take the thing seriously enough. "Writing," says Mary Roberts Rinehart, "in itself is sheer, grinding drudgery, and no innate literary impulse seeking expression can alter the fact." I hope I have not created any impression that I myself find writing books easy or a positive pleasure, or that I can do it on my head in my spare time. I drudge, then, at a built-in table in the alcove of my bedroom at the farm, a sort of annex to the big attic workroom because that is not on the furnace heating system and is often too chilly to be inviting, and the kerosene heater smells. As I have never achieved the art and the dignity of dictating for two or three hours after breakfast and then leaving the desk for the day with a satisfied conscience and a smug expression, I am likely to be there at any hour or all day if I can manage it.

The table faces a window towards the barnyard, with the big meadow and Haystack beyond—a noble scene in theory, but in 1948 it put the cement-mixer in my immediate fore-ground when they got round to that side, and gave me fair warning of all minor crises. Everything would be going along peacefully enough, my Corona in close harmony with the cement-mixer, when a sudden silence would fall outside, a trifle different in its feel from previous pauses in the day's activities. Then one of the four busy, easily moving figures would detach itself and start for the house, and my fingers would falter on the keys. Elmer's casual tones, drifting through the front screen door (always hooked, because of Che-Wee's suicidal impulses to follow anyone through any door rather than be left behind) and up the stairs, would be asking if the Boss was around. It might be only to say that someone was going into the village and did I want anything from the store. It might be that something had broken and might they order another—as though I would say No, you must do without! It might be that somebody had gouged a finger and the first-aid kit was wanted. Or it might be that a point had been reached in the reconstruction job where I had a decision to make or to revise. Whatever it was, it would detach me from my train of thought, and I sometimes had to make quite an effort to get aboard again, half an hour later. But even when a jack caught somebody's thumb there was no hurry or excitement, it was only that this time he was led in, dripping blood, and I didn't wait to be called.

You see what I mean. Bucks was nothing to it.

"But the writer has one practical obligation to himself," Miss Brittain continues briskly. "He must take all possible steps, once he has started work, to eliminate those extraneous interruptions which persons who are not authors are so ready to inflict on him. He can create his own mood by instituting regular hours of work and performing the external acts of concentration, but he cannot maintain that mood against all comers. . . ."

Well, there are those seven books, though I have no idea whatever when and how they got written. And of course we don't have to rebuild the barn every year. You mustn't think I'm complaining. . . .

Further as regards the manufacture of stories—some people seem always to resent a happy ending. I have had more objections from the critics than from readers about this habit of mine, and I have two main objections to their objections. If a book is a slice of life caught between cardboards, as I believe it ought to be, its boundaries set arbitrarily by the author although its characters have had an existence before it began and will go on living their lives after the final page is turned, then there is no such thing as a happy ending to a book any more than there is to a life until the character is ready to be buried. The girl may marry the man of her choice as the book ends—that seems to happen all round us every day, with few accusations from the Press of coincidence. Even then, it is sometimes a compromise—anywhere. I believe in giving my characters a reasonable chance to build a reasonable future, because most of the people I know or know about seem to achieve the same. But I give no written guarantee with any of my romances, since the characters are, I hope, pretty human. They're on their own from there on in. Secondly, people who have been consistently kicked in the teeth have a natural tendency to insist that life is like that. Some of them want to read about somebody who is a lot worse off than they are, because that makes them feel good. Some of them want to read about people who have what they haven't got because they like to imagine themselves in the place of some more fortunate character and derive comfort that way. These latter are sometimes contemptuously called Escapists, and are considered less than the dust intellectually. I don't know the right word for the former, but they like to call themselves Realists. Not long ago I came across what seemed to be the ultimate of this highly disillusioned condition, embodied in the concluding sentence of a signed review of a new novel. It read: *We may add that in this unusual novel final happiness is no detriment to realism.*

It is unprofitable to speculate about the people who cannot seem to digest what they refer to with disdain as a happy ending, but one does sometimes wonder what sort of company they keep. The fact remains that authors who permit a hero and heroine—for no one has invented less theatrical words for the principals in a romance—to stay in love long enough and hard enough to hurdle enough obstacles to marry each other at the end of the book, and without the prospect of having a child with two heads, are likely nowadays to be accused of a tendency towards rose-colored spectacles. Their output is not considered by some earnest thinkers to be sufficiently Cosmic. And yet, it's a funny thing, if what you see in the newspapers can be believed, something like that happens every day, right alongside the murders and the suicides and the divorces.

Doubtless now all the more elderly cynics in the audience will call me a Pollyanna. Remember her? Paul Gallico has pretty well disposed of the matter anyway, and in fewer words, by saying in his *Confessions*, "You tell me what's wrong with romance, and since when."

Shortening focus to a blank page which must be filled with words after a day of sun and wind and unaccustomed exercise, as happens to me during haying, is just as difficult as staying awake to write after overeating. I have tried everything—a drink before dinner, and no drink before dinner—a light meal of salad and fruit, and a hearty meat meal, eaten early and eaten late. It's still hard. Just as in the old days in the Museum Reading-room I used to try all the dodges I could think of to miss that inevitable middle-of-the-afternoon drowsy spell, and not all the changes I could ring on luncheon and tea ever saved me from it. Museum habitués are resigned to it, and you see them in all attitudes and phases of the cat-nap, up and down the rows of desks. There was one old gentleman who each afternoon put his head down on his arms and frankly snored for about ten minutes and then sat up, refreshed and brisk as anything, and went at it again. I never mastered his technique.

The long hot days on the farm followed one another, and it is nothing new for people writing about summer in the country to feel the need to ransack the thesaurus for words with which to paint the contentment and the beauty and the illusive peace of such a time. I know just enough not to try. But I will offer anyway a line from one of the many recent "family style" books which unless you were raised in a large, self-consciously comic family yourself, seem all pretty much the same. This one was embellished by a permanently ecstatic small boy who expressed his own unbearable elation in the triumphant statement: "This is a day I never saw before!" They were all days I had never seen before, and they were all delightful.

17.

$\mathcal{T}$REE SWALLOWS HAD
built again in the bird-house on the cedar tree at the end of the
porch above the lawn where we often have tea. We watched
the feeding of their brood as it grew. Then one day they had
all gone, and we said how clever the old birds had been to get
the family out and on the wing when nobody was looking, and
that presumably was that.

The next day one lone baby tree swallow was discovered
sitting in the middle of the road, unable to raise itself off the
ground, or feed itself, yelling hoarsely for the attention of its
vanished parents or some prowling cat.

I wanted a baby tree swallow even less than I had wanted

Che-Wee, because swallows are harder to feed, being insect eaters. Just about impossible to feed, in fact. But I picked the little foundling up and set him on the roof of the deserted birdhouse, not even sure that he was from the same brood, as the others had not been seen again. He was very weak and helpless, but he went on yelling feebly now and then, and a pair of old birds came and circled round him, trying to coax him into the air. But by now he was not strong enough to attempt to fly. I watched him all that afternoon, and they didn't once give him a morsel of food, though they returned two or three times to look at him. Maybe he wasn't even their own baby.

Realizing that if he was left there over night he would fall off and be dead by morning, I rang up Lee Crandall at the New York Zoological Park and asked him what to do about a tree swallow—Will being as far away as Venezuela and not consultable. Lee was not encouraging, but said to try him with boiled custard, unsweetened, and hard-boiled egg-yolk with breadcrumbs and codliver oil in it, and grasshoppers without their legs, cut up small. I tried the custard first, but he didn't like it much. I tried the egg-yolk and it came back up. It was too early in the season for grasshoppers where we were, and a search of the sunny knoll behind the house yielded just one small one. That went down and stayed, and he seemed brighter at once and obviously wanted more. When none was forthcoming, he soon faded again. The Coopers arrived with the milk, and we asked them if they had grasshoppers over their way and they promised to look.

Next morning he was still alive, in the little cage where I had perched him, but the custard didn't tempt him to open his mouth after the first taste. I put him back out on the birdhouse and he soon fell off, and no old birds came. In desperation I rang up the Park again, and they were very surprised at the lack of grasshoppers and suggested as a substitute scraped raw beef, scalded, and fed with forceps. Meanwhile the Coopers arrived with a few grasshoppers in a glass jar which they had found in front of their barn. The grasshoppers were very young and small and soft, and I cut them up smaller still and fed him and again he revived perceptibly. By alternating grasshoppers with the scraped beef I kept him alive that day. He sat on my finger with his eyes closed and wavered piteously, though he clung fast as to a friend, till I expected him to just keel over any minute. His eyes were sunken and half closed, and that is the worst sign.

When he was still alive the next morning I got just as stubborn as he was about it. Nobody thought I could raise him, including Lee Crandall, and this was just enough to make me decide that Poopy and I—he was all pooped out—would blooming well show 'em. I interrupted Elmer's work, even though it was the sacred Barn, and made him drive me over to the Coopers' and wait there while I crawled around on my hands and knees in the hot sun pouncing on minute grasshoppers and popping them into a glass jar with holes punched in the lid. Meanwhile the story had spread, and we had contributions from friends of the Coopers at the lake, and altogether we accumulated enough grasshoppers to last him a few more hours, and Elmer drove me home again.

The effect of proper food on Poopy was almost miraculous. His eyes came open, his voice got stronger, he really began to gain. I don't know how many trips I finally had to make to the Coopers' barnyard, nor why there should have been grasshoppers there and not on my own place unless because of their cattle, but for about a week I got nothing done beyond looking after Poopy. He learned to know me, and set up a yell for grasshoppers at sight of me, and finally made his first bumbling attempts to come *to* me for his food, instead of sitting with his face open, squawking. I knew then that we had turned the corner. Whatever I did, it was impossible to get *enough* grasshoppers, but the scalded meat kept him going between times.

The weather was fortunately very hot and sunny just then, and I perched him on a branch fastened to one of the posts of Che-Wee's screen porch, and gradually he began to preen himself a bit and take a little interest in life between feedings. Each time he had digested his meal and was perking up again for more, I would carry him into the long living-room and although he stuck to my fingers with desperate little claws like a burr I would toss him gently into the air and instinct would flap his wings in a descending curve to the sofa or love seat, where he landed soft and sat yelling till I collected him again. I would retrieve him at once, and toss him again, until we were both tired, and it was a great day when for the first time he turned in the air like a boomerang and flew back, still yelling, to my outstretched hand.

After we had played boomerang for a few days, the hand wasn't there any more, and he had to go on, frantically beating the air, to find another landing-place on the window-sill or top of the bookcase—and for the first time he now discovered that he could *lift* himself to a perch instead of always flying in a downward arc. This was progress. But the flying lessons went on, many times a day, till I saw the first sure effort at soaring.

By then he had learned to pick up his own food—first to take it himself from the forceps in my hand, then to take it from the table top, and finally to fly to me across the room, launching himself of his own accord from the security of a perch, to take it from a dish in my hand. He had begun to show definite affection, too, and wanted to sit on my shoulder— but unlike Che-Wee at any stage of his career, poor little

Poopy whiffed. It was not an entirely unpleasant odor, but it was a strong, acrid, pungent, musty whiff, either from the fact that he was a meat-eater, or that he had come from a nest of meat-eaters. And of course his droppings were many times as large and more frequent than Che-Wee's. He got quite handsome, though, as he learned to preen and his baby fluff gave way to feathers—a soft snowy white chest and dark, glossy back and wings. He had always the look of heavily padded shoulders, like a Varsity fullback, because his wings were so much larger in proportion than Che-Wee's, and his short legs and feet less in evidence.

The essence of a swallow's life is flight, and it would have been impossible to keep him healthy and properly fed for long. All that I ever hoped to do was to get him strong enough to fly and self-reliant enough to find his own food, and then his only chance was to set out into his world alone. A day or two before I had intended to turn him out, a pair of old birds appeared again over the back lawn, apparently attracted by his raucous little voice at feeding time on the porch. I caught him up and ran outside with him, loosened my fingers, and he took to the air like a breeze, strong and sure in his flight, circled several times above my head in a sort of salute, and was away to the top of a dead tree behind the house. It was very exciting to see him so confident, and we cheered him on, with a secret pang.

But the old birds, as was their exasperating habit, promptly disappeared again, and I wondered if I had been too soon. Poopy sat in the treetop for quite a while, and I stayed outdoors within sight of him, with the jar of grasshoppers in plain view, in case he wanted to come back. The old birds had never minded our presence before, and I didn't want to lose him yet, till I was sure he could stay up. I called to him now and then, and showed him the jar—he watched me, tempted, but independent. Then he made a few trial flights, as though half-minded to return to my shoulder, and I half hoped he would. Finally he took off, soaring, dipping, turning, soaring again, and vanished into the blue above the sugar-house.

I think he made it. Experienced bird men think he had a good chance. His own kind were not far away, if he wanted them. And he was certainly strong enough to fend for himself and had not been in the house long enough to lose all his instincts, and I had kept him out on the porch so that he was not too tender, as Che-Wee had soon become. At least he would have died if I had not taken him in and tried. I have no great belief in the infallibility of Nature and the legendary miraculous powers of the parent birds to do the right thing for a nestling in trouble—especially after the performance of that pair of old birds whose single-track avian minds could not reason that in order to fly a fledgling must be strong enough to try, and who were letting Poopy starve to death where he sat, apparently because in their calendar it was time for him to be on the wing. He may have been a hopeless little runt from the start, belated and underfed. Or he may have been from a totally different brood, hatched later. We will never know. And because I had no way to band him, we could never be certain, when the swallows returned to the bird-house in the spring, that he was among them.

Che-Wee, for one, was relieved to see the last of him, and had always left in a hurry when Poopy's blundering flights took him anywhere near the place where Che-Wee had planted himself to watch the living-room flying lessons. He seemed impelled to keep an eye on things there, perhaps out of jealousy, but would have nothing whatever to do with Poopy—perhaps because of the whiff. Oh, I forgot. The ornithologists have decided that birds have little or no sense of smell. And so how does Che-Wee know the difference, without tasting, between a teaspoonful of rum and water, which is sometimes offered as medicine, and a teaspoonful of fruit juice which is exactly the same color, and which he loves? *I* can smell the rum. So, I think, can he, because he refuses it. Cover the rum odor with orange juice—a dirty trick—and he will dip his beak trustfully. Just once. Then with much shaking of his head and wiping of his beak, he turns his back on the spoon. It is somehow not quite in character that Che-Wee is such a tee-totaller. He seems the sort of fellow that would like a nip now and then.

The brief sojourn of Poopy was inevitably followed by several days of anxiety when I asked myself if I should have brought him on a bit further before putting him out on his own, and cursed the old birds for making another frustrating appearance in time to force my hand. Coming on top of Petey's death, it also caused me to ask myself how I was going to evolve a philosophy adequate to deal with these little crises which were bound to occur perpetually if I allowed myself to become involved in the brief lives of pets and wild creatures. And while I never grudged Poopy the endless time it took to catch his grasshoppers and teach him to fly in the living-room, I was even now being thrown for a loss in my work by waging bitter war on Petey's mice and watching the sky for tree swallows and wondering. . . .

It was not by any means my old book-writing routine, near-sighted and content. Would I do better, perhaps, to retire again into my job and close the door of my consciousness to these gratuitous griefs and uncertainties and distractions, and—in a word—not just go out and look for trouble? But I knew very well that if I had tried to hypnotize myself into the fatuous belief that Poopy's parents would somehow accomplish his survival unaided, or to anaesthetize myself into the comfortable conviction that it was none of my business so long as I didn't actually *see* him die—which would certainly have saved a lot of trouble—I would still have been unhappy now, with a guilty conscience besides, for having shirked the issue and left it up to Nature or God, neither of which was doing very well by Poopy when I first saw him.

18.

*B*EFORE I HAD REACHED
any workable conclusion on the question, Che-Wee encountered what has come to be known as his Accident, and I was
stuck with the whole problem again, and with knobs on, because this time it was the one and only.

He was still not terribly fond of his screened porch, even
when it was not being used as a nursery for intruders who
smelled queer. That is, he preferred to be indoors if the family
were indoors. He used it as a vantage point from which to
survey our activities in the back yard, and not even the crack
of the .22 in our intermittent war with the red squirrels disturbed him there. Rather, he took a sporting interest in the
thing, and his attitude on the branch, crest erect, legs stretched,
chest out, expressed an almost audible, almost human, "Did
you get him?" each time the gun went off.

If the kitchen door was open at dusk he would still try to
go to sleep on the porch branch instead of in the kitchen win-

dow, and on warm nights we let him play Indians out there till after dinner, but he was always brought inside to his cage for the night. One evening we were all in the kitchen with the lights on, making drinks, and it had got quite dark outside, when Che-Wee suddenly shot into the room from the porch and flew head-on into the opposite wall and dropped to the floor. When I picked him up he got out of my fingers and flew blind into the window-pane. I got hold of him again, and there was a swelling the size of half a pea on his cheek under his right eye—pretty obviously a sting, particularly as wasps were swarming to a nest in the plant-house not far from the porch and had not yet been burned out. One must have been crawling about in the few leaves which still adhered to his branch, and either he had snapped at it for a fly or it had just plain stung something that moved. He was dazed and limp and in bad shape, but he could still sit up. Fortunately Will had returned by that time, and I had his experienced opinion that there was nothing any human being could do about it. He advised me to put Che-Wee in his sleeping-cage, cover him up, let him alone, and hope that he might sleep it off.

Determined not to make a fuss and play the fool, I did as he said, and then peeked surreptitiously several times that night and early in the morning, expecting to find Che-Wee wrong side up in the bottom of the cage each time I looked. But no, he stayed on his legs. Days went by, and still he stuck to his perch at night, and during the day sat about quietly on his window branches or a lampshade, made small, cautious flights, ate a little but without enthusiasm, and sported the most wonderful shiner a bird ever had. He was pretty sick, perhaps as much from concussion as from the sting. When the swelling began to go down the eye still looked bad, as though the pupil was either distended to the full size of the iris or reduced to a pinpoint, I couldn't be sure which. Before long it was plain that he couldn't see at all on that side, and it seemed to me that the eyeball was flattening.

On my next trip to New York I took Che-Wee in his travelling-cage to Dr. Foster, who put an ophthalmoscope on his eye and made a thorough examination. Harold Foster is an unusually large man, and he wore a circular mirror-thing on his forehead, and shot a light-beam into Che-Wee's face, while the nurse in a white uniform and the receptionist hovered sympathetically in the darkened consulting room. You might think an ounce of bird would have taken fright at such an experience. But Che-Wee had a self-possessed "Look, Doc, what happened to me" attitude about the whole thing which quite unnerved us all.

The wire of the cage got in the way of the light-beam and I took him out in my hand so the doctor could get the instrument closer to him, and he endured even that with composure, biting my fingers now and then to preserve face. When I set him back in the cage he shook himself briskly and his crest came up—"Well, that wasn't so bad!"

He now has his own typewritten card in the patients' file in Dr. Foster's office, with his case history, and at the end it says: *Prognosis for vision unfavorable.* But he still has one good eye, and there seems to be no reason to fear that the trouble will spread. The doctor prophesied cheerily that he would "Accommodate"—and that is what he has done.

A year later, his wings are as trimly crossed at the tips, his crest is as ready to rise, and he stands as high on his little stick legs, with his knickerbockers showing, as before his Accident happened. Will doubted if he would try to fly, for a bird has monocular vision and unlike a human being or a dog who loses one eye he is completely blacked out on one side of his head. But Che-Wee has never given up flying. His flights are shorter now, from here to there, and on to there, and sometimes he hovers like a hummingbird above his landing while he makes sure of it, but he has never fallen or bungled badly. Often after lighting he rubs the sunken eye against the perch in a patient, puzzled way as though trying to clear it, which is very hard for us to bear. But he can still spot an apple-seed way across the room, and he can still arrive neatly on your shoulder at breakfast, asking for orange-juice or shredded-wheat-and-cream out of your spoon.

He can see out of only one side of his head, and he can't solve it, but he has risen above it. Once more he is a lesson to humans. He is handicapped, but not afflicted. His courage and his unimpaired interest in life and food and friends and music out of the radio-box are equal to it. He is living his life as gracefully, serenely, and humorously now as before his Accident occurred.

Don't think for one minute that I am as philosophical as this sounds. There are still times when I could burst into tears against the unrelenting fact that his independence and his confidence and his gaiety are in any degree diminished by the injury. He never used to flinch from a movement of someone he knew, even if something passed over his head. But now, if I come in too suddenly on his blind side there is a startled instant, often not enough to drive him to flight, but enough to remind me. His trust reasserts itself at once, and he goes on eating or preening as before. Or I offer him food and he doesn't see it till I move it further in front of him. . . .

But he is too brave to be pathetic. His need of company seems greater now, and when I settle down to a spell of work

he knows the signs and comes to sit companionably on the arm
or the back of the big chair where I read, or on the lamp close
to my desk—so content just to be near me that I long for
something *more* to do for him. We play our little games. I
cover the meat of a sunflower seed or a broken piñon nut with
a leaf from the scratch pad and he takes the edge in his beak
and casts the paper aside with a flourish to snatch the treat
underneath. And often before anything has been hidden or
after the last morsel is gone he continues hopefully to tweak
at all loose papers, even tugging at the edge of the one I am
writing on, looking for buried treasure. And because I haven't
the heart to disappoint him forever, concentrated work is
considerably hindered. Or I pretend to catch his toes, till he
dances excitedly but without fear, and picks my fingers to
fend me off.

If the pen is out of the stand he likes to lick the ink off the
edge of the socket, standing on tiptoe on the onyx base to
reach. It can't be good for him, so I have to stop and insert a
twist of paper in the socket in place of the pen. This hurts his
feelings a bit, and he stands a moment gazing reproachfully at
the obstruction, before trotting on to the tray which holds
spare pencils and such, and soon has to be dissuaded from eating too much rubber eraser or lead. Next he will work a while
at the top of the glue-pot, his little pink tongue showing, till
I say, "*No*, Che-Wee, let it alone!" He pauses a moment again,
aware of the No, makes another pass or two at the glue, and
hops up on to the postal scales—one ounce, *that's* all right.
The telephone rings, and he flies down on to the cradle after
the receiver is removed, but he isn't heavy enough to break
the connection. From there he listens attentively to the conversation, and when dislodged at the end of it goes on busily to
his garden on the window-sill at the end of the desk, to get

171

a drink from the pool. Pretty soon something arrives lightly on my shoulder—*Teet?*—and fresh seeds must be tipped out into the dish, or an apple cut up for its seeds. . . .

This way we write books. The typewriter is another game. He rides on the carriage.

19.

*I*T WAS A GREAT YEAR for wild strawberries, because of all the rain, and I committed the crime of walking through hay which was almost ready to cut in order to gather them. Elmer bore it, but only just, remarking with visible forbearance that it was something his father never would stand for when they were kids. (Four small boys—you can hear it—"*Keep out of that hay!*") But apart from Che-Wee's daily treat, I gathered basketsfull, the largest wild strawberries I have ever seen, pale pink when fully ripe and very sweet. And I froze two cartons in the top of the refrigerator to make little shortcakes for Will when he came home.

His return was celebrated by suitable ceremonies in the newly finished barn room, and we sat there each twilight on the window-seat with his #7 binoculars, waiting for the deer to come into the meadow. They follow a regular beat, so that their path is plain through the hay, crossing from the barway on the road to the woods on the other side, and they usually appear well before dusk. Their tracks are often in the sandy ground around the barn in the morning, and more than once we have also found there the marks of a good-sized bobcat's pad. One morning I saw from an upstairs window what must have been a grey fox, though he looked as long-legged as a coyote, right in the barnyard barway, and I watched him lope away at his leisure across the field.

We put a windowsill feeder on one of the south windows of the barn room, and the usual skirmishing went on there fearlessly all day among the finches and all kinds of sparrows, within a yard of anyone who was writing at the work-table inside. Long as my association with naturalists has been, I still get a layman's perspective on their normal—to them —reactions to the unexpected appearance of a specimen. Such as the evening when I interrupted a long silence as Will and I sat reading after dinner in the living-room by saying, "Do *you* see something moving on the rug in front of the hearth?" If I had said, "Shall we go to town tomorrow?" or "What are you reading?" or even "Would you like a drink?" his answer would have been slow in coming, preoccupied, and possibly not much to the point. As it was, he sat up alertly, pulling in his legs, removed his reading-glasses, and peered at the floor in front of him with lively interest. "Nice little spider," he remarked comfortably then, and resumed his re-laxed posture, his glasses, and his mystery story, while the spider, which wasn't what I would call very little of its kind, made its unmolested way across the rug towards the dining-room. I have never myself had any prejudice against things that creep and crawl, which is fortunate, as I often suspect that his interest in living creatures increases proportionately with the number of legs they possess.

It was an English mystery story he read, as always, but this is not a form of Anglo-mania, merely a conviction arrived at from long experience that books written by Ngaio Marsh, Manning Coles, Anthony Gilbert, Patricia Wentworth, Margery Allingham, Agatha Christie—to name a few—are more to our taste in humor and background than the rough-and-tough American style. They are just more fun. (The same way that the crossword puzzles in the English periodicals are more fun, with their many anagrams, puns, and joking clues (*mother, on the whole = tomato*—ma, in toto!) than the flat-footed variety in our own papers.) And it is still hard to beat a good Oppenheim or A. E. W. Mason for rereading.

During the work on the barn, the tongue of the old wagon had snapped off, and no wonder, and we had to buy a new one —painted the bright John Deere green and yellow, with rubber tires, $148. It came in time to bring down the eight-by-eights and two-by-fours from the one-man lumber camp up the mountain. To ride on the springless wagon over a stony road was the finest shaking-up I ever had, but the view down the valley from the camp is magnificent. The wide hay-rack went on to the new wagon, and they started cutting, with still a different baler engaged this time, equally horrifying in its soulless efficiency, and another second-hand side-delivery rake, as our new one still had not come.

The results of fertilizing were very noticeable in the hay, even in a year which had begun badly for crops. The single swathe along the stone wall which had been purposely left for comparison was sparse and pale beside the new dark green growth which also showed a notable increase of red clover. As Old John still had no driving light, we used a rented jeep more than once and worked after dark to keep up with the baler and ahead of the weather. "Lazy folk work best, when the sun's in the west" was a proverb I first heard at this time, along with "Hay on Sunday, rain on Monday," which sounds more like a hex, but doesn't always work.

We had bought a new bush-and-bog harrow, painted red, to serve as both plough and harrow, and with it had extended the buckwheat field behind the house by as much again, and planted the ground where the buckwheat grew last year in corn and potatoes. I rode on the wide fender of Old John on its first day in the back field, and watched the brown, fragrant earth froth up behind the notched round blades like water round the prow of a ship. It weighs about 1200 pounds and Elmer says that it makes Old John sweat to haul it, and that when fully canted in wet earth it makes even T-20 beller a bit. Riding things just for the ride is always fun for me—I have ridden the mowing-machine, the fertilizer spreader, the side-delivery rake, and the stone-boat besides the tractors and the dreigh—when Elmer says "Hang on!" and throws in the clutch the result is often rather like the Bermuda crossing in the equinox, but you have more chance to get off and walk.

During the preoccupation with The Barn a sudden visitation of potato-bugs got a start on us and I undertook to deal with them myself. Our usual method in the smaller garden had been to take a can of kerosene and a stick and poke them off the leaves into the can. But some of them always missed the can and fell on the ground, and it was slow, back-breaking work. With many times as many plants to do in the back field, I soon discarded the stick and used my fingers, which wasn't pleasant at first with the soft ones, but I got used to it, and it was certainly much faster and fewer of them got away. The potato crop was not seriously damaged, and Will was busy with a potato hook and a wheelbarrow for days when he innocently volunteered to dig them. We take instant and unfair advantage of all such unwary offers.

Both the tractors now got a new coat of paint, to stop the rusty places, and Elmer did a neat job of re-upholstering on T-20's seat with an old tarpaulin, and gave him a thorough overhauling in his stall under the barn. It was the first real doctoring he had required since he came to us.

Along about the first frost the new side-delivery rake arrived at last, the usual bright John Deere green and yellow—and was unloaded in pieces and stowed under the barn till next season. It is *not* a lovable piece of machinery any way you look at it, but very essential to haying and still as scarce as hen's teeth, either new or second-hand. Essential because everybody needs it at the same time, and needs it urgently, so that to rent or share one only leads to complications. With luck you can accommodate yourself to the baler schedule, and to own a baler for a small place is sheer swank, at a cost of around $2000. But you do need your own mowing-machine, rake and wagon in order to meet the baler schedule. This equipment, new, comes to around $650. Plus the wheeled tractor.

By no means all of the wooden buckets had got painted the season before, and some had been painted only on the inside, owing to pressure of other work. The painting job includes a tightening of the hoops, which is done by laying a chisel against the hoop's lower edge and knocking it with a hammer

—very tedious and noisy, but the hoop moves up as much as half an inch sometimes, tightening the seams. This autumn the stack of fertilizer bags by which I had heretofore mounted to the barn loft was replaced by a permanent ladder—one of the vertical built-on kind which are my idea of a death-trap and which I shall never learn to use without reluctance and a conviction that I am going to fall off backwards and break everything that holds me together. We used aluminum paint, which spreads like magic, dries very fast, lasts longer than the other, and looks beautiful. So again the year had come full circle and I was in the barn loft painting buckets—insides first, then turn them upside down on the sawhorse and do the bottom, then the outsides in two rounds from the top down, lift them by the lower edge and stack them, still wrong side up, alternately on the bottoms of the row below, in a gleaming pyramid. Using aluminum paint, a bucket can be done all at once, without waiting for the inside to dry for a day.

We ordered new spouts, to cut down leakage from old bent ones, and to get a handier kind without a loose ring and hook. And bang went most of the year's profits again, but equipment has to be invested in. The gathering-tub also got a coat of aluminum paint inside, and barn-red outside, and the arch in the sugar-house was aluminumed against rust, and we began to look rather spruce. A loft had been built into the sugar-house to store the buckets in—when I bought the place they were piled on the damp earthen floor, which was one thing that was the matter with them, and they had spent the past winter in the barn loft, which was inconvenient.

When it was time for me to return to New York before Thanksgiving we had still not got to the bridges on the sugar-roads, and I was sorry to miss that, along with further alterations to the sugar-house which would move the door and let in more light, and house the storage tank under its own lean-to outside so that the steam from the pans couldn't reach the sap. We did get down to one job we had been looking forward to, and that was blasting some of the rocks out of the upper hay-field beyond the barn.

The eternal Fourth of July latent in every American cosmos brought broad grins at the prospect to the faces of everybody on the place, including the visiting Carlisles, who laid hold of spade and crowbar with joy, and Kay burrowed like a woodchuck digging at the holes in the exact spot chosen by Elmer for the charges. When the hole was almost ready he would cut a slit in the dynamite sticks and insert the little red and yellow wires. Then would come the pause of achievement and everybody watched while he went flat on his stomach to push the charge down the hole, and we all handed in clods to pack it down, and then retired to a respectful distance.

Will had presented us with the historic plunger which had set off his underwater charges in his diving days in Haiti and Bermuda, when he fished with a dynamite cap on the end of a pole instead of a hook, and it operated at the end of 50 yards of rubber-covered wire. The boom-boom game never palls, and no guest ever fails to fall under its foolish enchantment, standing about in any kind of weather enthralled by each new rock as its turn comes.

Some of the rocks were several feet across and they either lay on top as glacial deposit or sent their roots down towards China as part of the original Vermont, and it was not always possible to guess which before the first charge went off. They either rolled over as neatly as a flapjack, or they splintered into soaring chunks, according to their nature. Sometimes more than one charge was needed to level off below the surface. And the resulting crater was endlessly interesting each time.

Every rock which is eliminated speeds up the mowing and lessens the chance of delay from a broken Pitman-rod, even if it weren't such fun to watch. And when the pieces are out on top, T-20 bustles up with the stone-boat, drags the rocks on to it with his winch and logging chains, and removes them to the big rock dump in the middle of the field or to the place behind the barn where we are extending the stone wall. Fortunately for the entertainment of visitors, to say nothing of ourselves, there is no sign of running out of rocks.

Each winter the place is invaded by men in trucks who want to buy Christmas trees, and each winter the answer is the same —No. If Elmer were not there to say it, the chances are that a number of trees would quietly disappear, and no one might be the wiser, though the penalty for pirating trees is very severe. There is no good reason why we should not sell some trees, as the growth up the hill is much too thick for its own good. Sometimes, riding on the dreigh along the upper roads during a wooding job, I think, There, we could certainly spare some of those. But the little trees look so happy and trustful in their colonies that I haven't the heart. And so we continue to be creeping with Christmas trees, and not even one cut for our own use, for we are always in New York in December.

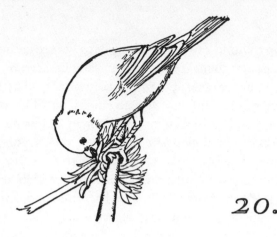

20.

I HAVE SIMPLIFIED THE Vermont-New York luggage situation so far as possible by having doubles and understudies of everything I own, from clothing and cosmetics to reference books and typewriters, so that in theory I can travel between the two houses with nothing but a hand-bag, and find everything I need at either end. Like most theories, it sounds fine but it doesn't work. For one thing, I can never be separated from the perpetual unfinished script which is an albatross around every author's neck. And a script always has friends and relations in the shape of little notebooks and big source books without which it cannot progress. The master-copy, with its pencilled interlining and scribbled notes on bits of loose paper, and the handwritten notebooks, representing accumulated hours of labor, are much too irreplaceable to be trusted to the mail or even to a checked bag—the nightmare story of the maidservant who used the doubtless dilapidated-looking manuscript of Carlyle's *French*

Revolution to build a fire with in the days before carbon copies existed is enough to make any writer wake up screaming. . . .

At this point it occurred to me to wonder what the basis and source of that literary legend might be. The particular volume I needed to look it up in is not in duplicate and was in New York. It's always the only one you haven't got that you want. So I wrote to Marion King at the Society Library, and here, with her permission, is her reply, which arrived by return mail: "John Stuart Mill, who had collected many books on the French Revolution, was eager to help Carlyle with his history of it. Carlyle set to work at once and finished the first volume in five months, and lent the MS to Mill, who left it at the house of a Mrs. Taylor who had separated from her husband on account of her intimacy with Mill. There it was burned accidentally, according to Mrs. Taylor, and Carlyle who had no copy and few notes had to write it afresh. Mill sent a check for £200 as compensation. Carlyle accepted only £100, the actual cost of living while he was writing what had been burned. —Do you want more than that?"

Well, no, though it certainly opens up endless speculation, and is much more interesting than my original impression that it was Carlyle's own servant who had made the mistake. It also illustrates the way the Library functions for its members. I have a confession to make now. The information was found in the Britannica, and I have a set of that on my shelves here and didn't consult it!

Throughout all the summers in England and the countless trips to Bermuda and California and Williamsburg and hither and yon, my current manuscript has relentlessly accompanied me, weighing roughly a ton, in a bag which I myself carried by hand and never lost sight of. I'm never sure it's worth all the trouble, but at least it's all I have to go on with, and if I lost it I might doubt still more the necessity to try to recon-

struct it as Carlyle had to do. It is even harder to love a manuscript in its early or mid-stages than it is to dote on the finished
product. It would never take much to call the whole thing
off, so I treat them tenderly lest the fragile idea just come
apart in my hand before I get it on paper. When it is done it
is the best I can do, and I leave it to stand on its own legs somehow, and begin to worry about the next one. The next one,
like the poor, always we have with us.

So a stout Gladstone bag which will hold all my book-
writing tools except a typewriter is an inseparable travelling
companion. And then there is Che-Wee's little zipper bag
which contains him in his travelling-cage and his own personal
luggage—a box of seeds and an apple for the journey, a teaspoon for drinks along the way, and his silver porringer. And
that too is never out of my hand. Now, in addition, we had
another bag with two more travelling-cages, containing two
canaries.

The bird I got to take Petey's place for Elmer's mother was
an enchanting olive green creature with a yellow breast. He
was one of those born clowns that occur in the world of pets
the same as among humans. He hung upside down on the bars
to eat his apple slice, which he could have reached with less
trouble from the perch. He would stretch up and catch the
wire of his swing in his beak and pull it towards him, let go,
and watch the pendulum swing with a never-failing pleased
surprise. His voice was an excited, ingratiating "*See?*" as if he
were saying, "Look—no wings!" If we hadn't got him out
of the house quick we couldn't have let him go, and he hadn't
been in her kitchen ten minutes before he began to take a bath
in his water-cup to amuse her, and accepted a saucer of water
without hesitation and washed himself delightedly in a perfectly strange room as though he had lived there always.

Our own house seemed a little quiet when he had gone, for

Che-Wee is not a talkative bird. Then when the Accident occurred I prepared to follow my own stoic advice to other people and have another bird ready to take his place—so far as any bird could—if I lost him altogether. So I got a little yellow female with olive markings direct from a breeder, thinking she would be healthier and tamer than a bird out of a shop. She was neither. She had a cough when she came, and she was frightened stiff to be alone in a cage. We called her Budge, for Fussbudget, and when we let her come out and fly around the room Che-Wee let it be clearly understood at once that he was not going to be imposed on by any girl canary. After a few days I decided to send her back and get a more sophisticated bird from a shop, who had got used to people approaching the cage and wouldn't go into fits when it was time to change the paper each morning. There was only one green one, where I went that time, and I had no leisure to hunt round. The cages were not well kept there, and I did what I always advise everyone never to do, I bought a bird in poor plumage out of a dirty cage—in order to have a green one, as I was convinced that they had more sense than the yellow ones. It was very young and *very* small, its sex was undetermined, and it wasn't guaranteed to sing. It cost $2.98 against Budgie's $5, but when I got it home and put it in a big cage I knew I had got a Bird.

Bitsy—he has never grown—is olive green with barred wings and an orange breast, and has an orange overtone in a bright light. At the back of his minute head where he can't see them are two tiny pale yellow feathers, like a hair-ribbon. He has an alert, knowing, rather satirical face, and great self-possession, like a child which has come up the hard way on the wrong side of the tracks. His voice is likely to be a bit hoarse, as though he had been at the gin again. And as I might very well have anticipated from his condition when I bought him, he is permanently Delicate, and makes any amount of extra trouble.

His feathers were in such bad shape, from the dirty cage, that I had to take him in my hand and clean them and his long, fragile feet, in warm water. He hated this, and screamed with fury when my fingers closed round him—temper, not fear. Then, as it was no use, he gave himself up for dead and hung his head limply, eyes half closed, feet inert, till I almost wondered if I *had* squeezed him. Compared to Che-Wee, who is a solid little chunk of bird, he felt the size of a bumble-bee in my hand. When I put him back on the perch he sat there a while, rumpled and damp and disgusted, and finally began in a resigned sort of way to preen himself. In a few days he condescended to take his own baths and then his appearance improved.

Meanwhile, Budgie had fallen in love with him, and was perfectly quiet and contented now that he had come to live with us, so I hadn't the heart to send her away. She would try to snuggle up to him with little kissing motions, which he endured rather than encouraged, and to which he made very little response. Budgie's whole personality was blonde, and she bored Bitsy and Che-Wee inexpressibly with her flirtatious ways. Meanwhile too it became fairly certain that Che-Wee was not going to die and that his eye had healed and would not bother him much. So all of a sudden I seemed to have three birds. But at least the other two regarded a cage as home, and stayed in it without any sense of confinement, returning to it of their own accord after brief outings around the room.

During the winter Budgie's cough got steadily worse, and her beautiful plumage began to deteriorate, and I had to send her back for treatment to the place where she came from. I received in exchange another golden female with a coquettish olive cap and shawl. Bunty arrived in the breeding season, two years old, and very anxious. The fact that Bitsy was not old enough to know what it was all about didn't stop her from pursuing him shamelessly, till I kept them in separate cages in different rooms. But Bunty's maternal instincts never waned, and she kept up a perpetual flutter of her wings and nervous, pleading chitter. They assured me it wouldn't last, but it did.

We brought her with us when we came up at sugaring time and learned that Leon and his wife had a male canary, also feeling the spring. So Bunty went down to Leon's house and married Dicky and laid five eggs in the nest Mrs. Leon gave her. They were sterile. After a little while Mrs. Leon let her try again, with the same result, and Elmer began to make unkind remarks to Leon about his rooster.

The saga of the canary I sent to Elmer's mother has become a masterpiece of straight-faced lying. It began one day when we were all in the kitchen during the lunch-time lull and I called attention to Bitsy's trick of pinning a piece of grass or celery leaf to the perch with one foot and eating between his toes. It's really quite a thing, to see him carry up in his bill something almost as big as he is from the bottom of the cage to the perch and then firmly place one foot on it to hold it there while he eats. "My mother's bird," said Elmer casually, "takes it up in his fist like this." And he bent an elbow monkey-wise. We laughed. A few days later he noticed me setting out Che-Wee's glass bath-dish on the kitchen sink. "My mother's bird," he remarked, "draws his own bath." A few days after that I said skeptically, "I suppose your mother's bird is singing by now?" He appeared to consider. "I don't know," he said, and added with perfect theatrical timing, "but he plays the piano." This sort of thing went on until finally after Bunty's second disappointment he announced that his mother's bird had laid an egg, all by himself. This seems to be the truth, for once, but by now we can't be sure.

Bitsy has proved to be even more of a Character than I suspected from the first. His repertoire of Geisler's remedies resembles an elderly invalid's bedside collection. He catches cold very easily and wheezes, and has to have Cold-aid in his drinking water, and a bit of cotton soaked with Inhalant in the bottom of his cage at night. One of his back toes has a tendency to get inflamed and he has to be caught and have his foot soaked in boric acid and painted with special foot ointment. He is kept on a strict diet, but even then a little too much greens can bring on interior difficulties and he has to have Digestive-aid in boiled drinking water. No ailment lasts long if promptly treated, but the intervals are painfully brief. "Bitsy's in trouble again," is too often heard at cage-cleaning time in the morning, and the right medicine is resignedly administered. Unlike Che-Wee, he rather enjoys his medicines. Drinking-water colored pink or brown is apparently more interesting than plain white water, and he sips with visible relish and is soon visibly improved. He has no hypochondriac tendencies, he merely plays in hard luck, with a pathetic cheerfulness in the midst of affliction, and a bright eye cocked to see what remedy he will get next. And he stays unbelievably small for so much personality. His feet are so long for his size that when he stands flat on a table he looks as though he was wearing snowshoes. His plumage will never be quite right till he has moulted again, and he wakes up each morning with a sort of tousled look, as though he had burrowed all night in the bedclothes. He sleeps in his swing, and in the evenings he goes up into it and sits there firmly when he considers that he has had enough of his day, waiting with a kind of aggressive patience to be covered up for the night.

He likes to come out of his cage and fly around after Che-Wee, and he wants to light on our shoulders and eat at the table with us as he sees Che-Wee do, but still doesn't quite dare. Che-Wee behaves towards him like a rather tough big brother. If he feels good-natured he will allow Bitsy to approach gingerly and feed from the far edge of the dish he is using—but he is likely at any moment to make a threatening motion with his beak to drive him off. Peck-dominance in the home, this is. Bitsy is so philosophical about it, you want to bop Che-Wee. Bitsy waits a while and then valiantly tries again, and sometimes is allowed to stay. He likes to sit near Che-Wee on the window branches, but is not permitted to come *too* near. Like a faithful little shadow he will preen when Che-Wee preens, eat what Che-Wee eats—even if he can only have what's left after Che-Wee has finished—and bathe when Che-Wee bathes, accepting humbly the water which remains in the dish when Che-Wee has done splashing, if there is no one there to freshen it for him. We have set two dishes side by side, and Bitsy still prefers the one Che-Wee has used. You can't feel too sorry for him because he has such a good time out of life anyway, and living is so perpetually exciting to him, and the small pleasures which come his way are all so wonderful. He has such equanimity, as though he knew things, at his age, that a lot of people never learn.

Che-Wee remembered Christmas. The year before, we had tied up a couple of tiny parcels in white tissue paper with narrow red ribbon, and after only a little rehearsal he learned to tweak the end of the ribbon till the single knot gave and the present shook loose and appleseeds or sugar crumbs spilled out of the paper. When we began to wrap parcels a year later nobody but Che-Wee remembered this accomplishment until he rushed down to the bridge table among the tissue paper, ribbons, and seals, and began pulling the ends of all the ribbons on all the parcels, regardless of their size, looking for the one which belonged to him. And so he had to have a Christmas present himself every time we wrapped up other people's from then on till December 25th, when he received the usual piñon nut, appleseeds, and a small gold pill-box with bits of rock candy rattling about inside. If you shake it, he dances with impatience till it is opened for him to select just one crumb.

People without experience of birds and no particular love of pets will doubtless by now consider me quite besotted. I myself used to think that I could do without such embellishments to an already crowded life. But as the world grows grimmer and greyer, and the toll of the years goes on among one's friends, the confident insouciance and unconscious humor of something live and busy about the room, something utterly one's own as even children cannot be for long, is very sustaining. And a tame bird has learned one of the most invaluable things you can contemplate nowadays—not to be afraid.

21.

$\mathcal{T}$HE WINTER WAS MILD
and spring was early in 1949, and sugaring weather began in
February. As I had not been able to run up during the winter,
even for a few days, I was very pleased to pack up the birds
and Mother and set off a good two weeks earlier than we had
expected to. Will was to follow within a week, when everything would be under way, and we were ambitious to give

him the whole show before he took off for a flying visit to Trinidad.

There was still over a foot of snow when we arrived, the sun was shining, the roads were muddy, Leon was already at work in the sugar-house, and Elmer was battling some obscure cold virus which would not depart after a decent interval of bed and care, but allowed him to stay on his feet and do the job by main force. The arch in the sugar-house was levelled off and the pans set, and the remodelling had been done, so that the forty-barrel storage tank now lived in its own lean-to built on at the back with a door between it and the steam from the boiling, which would keep the sap cool and improve the color of the syrup. The door in the front of the sugar-house had been moved, so as not to interfere with the draft when it was opened, and there was now room below where the tank had been to set up one of the famous little stoves made out of an oil barrel, with its pipe joining the main one from the arch, for heat when the fire in the arch was not burning.

It represented an enormous amount of work, in the removal and replacement of the back wall of the sugar-house, and the shift of the heavy tank to its new quarters. Elmer and T-20 had done it between them, with no other assistance, no one will ever know quite how. "T-20 had hold of one end of the eight-by-eight," Elmer said when I asked him, "and I had hold of the other." And the first boiling proved the wisdom of the change, for the color was "light fancy" and the flavor matched it. We have never had trouble with flavor, even late in the season, but the syrup had heretofore been a little dark for the fashion.

The day after we arrived was warm with a pale sun, and they scattered buckets on the lower lot and tapped there. I rode on the back of the dreigh on the bucket towers, and the trees are so close to the road down there that Leon sat on the front bar and sailed the buckets out into the snow where they landed neatly, usually wrong side up as they should be, at the base of their trees. "These buckets got wings!" he remarked in pleased surprise and with a remarkably good aim. And Elmer, taking him unawares with a sudden shout and peremptory pointing finger at a tree which was without a bucket, reflexed him into lobbing a hasty one without looking, and thus accomplished again the perennial, ever-new joke of the sugar-lot, and the triumphant, jeering, "Soft ma-ple! Soft maple!" To bucket a soft maple, much less to tap one, is not to know beans when the bag is open. Leon was just as tickled as anybody, and said "Dawg-*gone!*" and dropped off the dreigh to retrieve his bucket. Things are very funny, and it is very easy to laugh, when the snow has begun to melt and the sap is running, and everybody clowns a bit. In place of Phil, who had fulfilled his expressed intention of going into the Navy, we had Roy, who not long ago was one of the several small boys who mowed our lawn in a rather indifferent way, and who had almost overnight developed into a handy young man, cheerful to have around, and rugged too—it takes a good deal of heft to sling gathering pails around all day. Coming down hill on the way home with a full tub, Roy still had enough energy and spirits to drop off the back end of the dreigh, Indian through the evergreens beside the road at double time, and "Boo!" at T-20's stolid progress at some unexpected point further on. Elementary humor though it might be, it was always good for a laugh just because everybody felt so good and the sap was running again.

Then we had "sugar snow"—so called not because it looks like sugar, but because it is a wet, heavy snow which falls in big flakes and means good sugaring weather—and tapping went on all over the place like mad. Will arrived on a gathering day, and went as it were straight from the train into an alpaca-lined jacket, high galoshes, and the Sears Roebuck deer-stalker's cap that makes him look like Sherlock Holmes's kid brother, and out into the lower lot, where he lugged a gathering pail with the rest of them. The next day he saw that sap boiled, and the day after that he ate it on waffles and seemed to find very little wrong with it.

Always baffled by machinery in any form, but at the same time always unwillingly fascinated by it, he found the evaporator an endless source of worry because he didn't understand exactly *how* it worked and why it behaved as it did. And as soon as he began to ask questions and doubt the answers, I couldn't see either, though until then I had accepted the brief explanation—Gravity—at its face value and given it no further thought. Will knew what gravity was, all right, better than I did, but it didn't suit him as an explanation. One of the nicest chapters he ever wrote is in *Jungle Peace* and has to do with the recurrent, accusing note of a great black frog in a Guiana swamp who said *"Wh-y?"* at him until it induced a mood of philosophical despair at the smallness of his cosmic knowledge. Nearly thirty years later in a Vermont sugarhouse he raised the same simple, exasperating query, and was no better satisfied with the answers he got there.

Like mathematics and some of the larger universal concepts, it makes perfect sense while it is being explained, and then begins to go fuzzy at the edges as soon as you let go of it. In words of one syllable, it seems to be something like this: The sap goes from the storage tank down a hose to Regulator #1, which is in a small pan set on the back pan. Here it is slightly warmed before it travels through a pipe to Regulator #2, whose float regulates the depth of the boiling sap throughout

the whole pan—just under two inches. From here it passes
into the flues of the back pan, boiling hard, and on through an
open passage into the front pan, which lies directly over the
fire and is divided into four lengthwise sections with three
open gates at opposite ends. The pan is laid exactly level on the
arch, and the fourth and last gate is closed by a hand-operated
plug. When the sap in the fourth partition reaches syrup consistency (211°) it is drawn off into a bucket through an outside faucet and the hand-plug at the other end of the partition
is removed at the same time to admit more sap to replace the
syrup passing out of the tap. If it does not come in fast enough
the pan will scorch and there is heck to pay. As the sap flows
from the third partition into the last one, to replace the drawn
off syrup, it lowers the level in all the sections behind it, so that
Regulator #2 automatically opens and allows fresh sap to
restore the level through the pan. In other words, gravity. I
hope this is clear?

While Will was still here we had a blizzard—a real one, with
a howling wind and all the trimmings. We burned white birch
logs in the fireplace, logs cut from damaged trees on our own
hillside the summer before, and did the wicked cross-word
puzzles in the English *Country Life*, and were immensely cosy,
and T-20 got out his pusher and opened up the roads, and
Will saw more snow than he had seen since his Jersey boyhood
—and in spite of his phobia for cold weather he rather enjoyed
himself. But the half-boiled sap standing in the back pan began
to freeze deep and had to be warmed up and drained, and what
little sap there was in the buckets froze solid. Still, he had seen
sugarin', and when he left he took with him some syrup which
he had personally escorted from the tree to the can. By the
time he reached Trinidad by air, we were down to zero in
Vermont. When it did warm up there was no damage done,

and we made more and better syrup than any year heretofore. It is pleasant to show progress with each succeeding year according to plan.

Then to everyone's consternation, Elmer's virus took a new lease on life, and after he had boiled all one day with a personal temperature of 102°—before I stuck a thermometer in his mouth—he went home to bed and was ordered by his doctor to stay there, and barely missed bronchial pneumonia. Leon and I pottered around for a whole day, feeling lost and depressed and thinking things over, but we both knew we were going to boil down that remaining half tank of sap ourselves. He cut some wood and brought it down, to fill in the time—I drifted uneasily around the house—the news from Elmer was not encouraging, and he couldn't even get to the phone to tell us what to do—heck, we said, let's boil. So long as we don't burn the pan, we said.

And we made syrup. About all I did was skim, and lend moral support when it came time to draw off, but we made stuff that was right on the red line of the hydrometer, and it tasted and smelled just like syrup. It was darker than Elmer's, because the sap had stood a day in the tank and because we didn't dare boil as fast as he did—and because it was getting late in the season and wasn't freezing properly at night. We were all day at it, and in a perspiration most of the time, and we needed a drink when we finished. But what we made tasted all right on waffles.

Meanwhile in the coolish weather sap was dribbling into the buckets, and standing there turning a little milky, and Elmer is a fanatic about clean buckets. Unless the old sap was emptied out on to the ground before the next run it would pollute the fresh clear stuff we still hoped to get. Elmer, croaking down the telephone, said for Leon to "get out his horse"—T-20—

195

and go round the whole lot and empty the buckets. This could hardly be done in one day by one man, so I offered to go along and do what I could, as the buckets would not be full enough to bother me with their weight. They weren't full on the lower lot which we did in the morning, but after luncheon we went up the hill, and there the drip had been steadier, so that when I had begun to flag a bit we found the buckets as much as half full. It all had to be dumped, for the sake of the fresh run, but unhooking and tipping metal buckets which are even half full is a little more than I would choose to do very long on the tired end of the day. I knew that Leon had begun to watch me for signs of fatigue, and I was willing that he should by covering twice as much ground as I did empty the ones on the high ledges where you had to climb and balance to reach them. But I lasted out the day, and was none the worse for it after a night's rest.

Then there was another run and gathering, and that wasn't so funny. The weather had gone back on us, and what we made was no longer a fancy shade, though it was good barrel syrup, which is graded and sold to candy and tobacco makers, and as we were getting similar reports from other sugar lots we didn't feel too incompetent. We built Elmer a new plank floor in the sugar-house for a Surprise, and cleaned out the pans and the storage tank for the next run before he could tell us to on the phone. When he finally did come back, with his bronchial tubes still playing tunes in the stethescope, we were making good barrel syrup, though sugarin' was about over. Just as snow-fleas at the beginning of the season are a sign of a warm-up and a good run, spiders and moths in the tree-buckets mean an end.

Once again the season could hardly be called a good one, like the old days, for we had lacked the freezing nights and warm sunny days which bring the best runs, and existed instead in a sort of coolish monotone. On advance commitments we could have sold twice as much syrup as we made, which was a left-handed sort of satisfaction at best. Already our thoughts turned ahead to next year. The new spouts were wonderful and leakage had been almost eliminated. We could use still more, and more metal buckets, for young trees have come to tapping age, up the hill, and a new road would open up another whole circle. Clearing and thinning must go on all summer, as the wood was gathered—mud holes must be corduroyed—the sugar-house lean-to must be filled again with wood for next year's fires. . . .

It is endless but entrancing work, because it is work that is half a game, done on your own time, in hot sun and woods shade, with the mountain beyond. Well, no, it wasn't a top season this year. We didn't make much money, but we had a lot of fun.

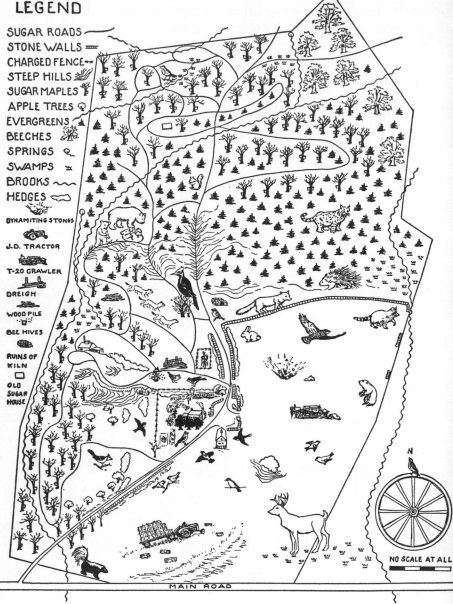

LEGEND

SUGAR ROADS
STONE WALLS
CHARGED FENCE
STEEP HILLS
SUGAR MAPLES
APPLE TREES
EVERGREENS
BEECHES
SPRINGS
SWAMPS
BROOKS
HEDGES

DYNAMITING STONES
J.D. TRACTOR
T-20 CRAWLER
DREIGH
WOOD PILE
BEE HIVES
RUINS OF KILN
OLD SUGAR HOUSE

N

NO SCALE AT ALL

MAIN ROAD

198

22.

EVER SINCE IT BECAME
known that I was writing this book I have been warned again
and again that after it is published we will be overrun by total
strangers in cars who want to see the place with their own eyes
and ask personal questions. This is indeed a doleful prospect for
people who have always preferred that even their closest

friends should telephone before ringing the doorbell, even in New York, and who are seldom pleased by unannounced arrivals of any description. I can only hope that the prophets of doom are wrong, because now the book is written and I had fun doing it and hope it will be fun to read.

The place isn't easy to find and we like it that way, and there isn't anything special to see when it is found—an ordinary white New England house with three maple trees in front of it, a big red barn set on a slope with hayfields all around. Nothing is visible of sugaring and haying except for the actual brief season, when everyone is overworked and preoccupied. Che-Wee is shy of visitors who stand about with their hats on waiting for him to do something funny. I am still trying to write books.

Midway of our seventh summer in Vermont I have just drawn a long breath and looked round. The snowballing expenses of the first years have at last begun to shrink—though the taxes have more than doubled. Our necessary equipment is bought and paid for, fuel storage tanks are buried and filled, the minimum basic household comforts are achieved. Our sugaring outfit only wants expanding, our wage bill is static at five or six weeks of extra help for sugaring and one week for haying. No more barn jobs loom.

Che-Wee's screen porch at the back has been built in permanently with a glass end towards Haystack and the prevailing winds, and it also serves as an ideal nursery and hospital for other bird foundlings in which he takes no interest whatever. Two young purple finches were rescued from the lawn in one week this summer, one apparently stunned from flying into a car fender, one dazed and weak and starved after cold, wet weather which had brought on a terrible case of diarrhea. The first regained the use of his wings after a few days' rest and feeding in safety, and was banded on the right leg and set on his way. The second stayed for two weeks or more, regaining his strength and weight, and then was put out with a band on his left leg. Both have been seen many times since, in perfect condition and holding their own in the perpetual feeder squabbles. Neither of them ever showed any fear of a hand or of being inside a house, and after flying against the inside of the screen a couple of times accepted it as a natural barrier and lived and fed and preened behind its protection, contentedly hopping and flying from branch to branch within sight of their friends and relations outside. An exceptionally hot dry summer made it possible for them to stay out of artificially heated rooms and so they did not become tender and subject to chill as Che-Wee of necessity did during his infancy. The second finch as it got better showed a tendency to dispute ownership of a branch or a seed dish with Che-Wee, who was outraged at these intrusions and chittered angrily if his territory was encroached on. I was worried over the handicap of his blind side, which made it impossible for them to fight it out on equal terms, and always stood ready to interfere on his behalf. Within two or three days peck-dominance was established, and the younger bird gave way peaceably before the righteous indignation of the owner of the porch, just as Bitsy does.

Both orphans were considerably older than Che-Wee was when I adopted him, and were able to pick up their own food from the beginning, as he was not. A third finch youngster from the second hatching appeared as late as August with an injured wing which would not allow him to rise a foot off the ground when I picked him up under the feeder. His appetite was good and again there was no fear of a hand. He preferred to sit on my wrist than not while I cracked sunflower seeds for him, and fed from my fingers at once, and allowed me to pick him up in my hand at any time, which Che-Wee has never permitted, although he is willing to step up on a proffered finger and perch there. The wing was slow to strengthen, and I tried tossing him gently towards the living-room sofa as I had done with Poopy, until gradually he was able to keep himself in the air and at last to lift himself in flight to a higher perch than his starting level. Finally he too went out on his own, wearing a little bracelet with a recorded number. Each of the three had a distinct personality, the last one the most appealing, but none of them stayed with us long enough to forget their bird ways or to quite break our hearts at parting. I am afraid ingenuity gave out and they were all called Junior. One reason for the number of foundlings this year, I think, is the increase in the number of finches. Apparently everybody who was born here last year has returned with his mate to raise his own family.

The latest addition to the asylum was a very young thing my laundress brought to me for rearing. I was not sure what he was, but she had picked him up in the edge of the village with no visible adult birds about. The shape of his bill indicated the fly-catcher persuasion, and the old grasshopper hunt began again. They were very plentiful this year, little soft ones. He thrived on the diet, and enjoyed his meals of chopped grasshopper alternating with Geisler's Canary Egg-biscuit soaked in warm milk, and hard-boiled egg-yolk mashed up with toast crumbs. Although he showed no fear, he had an aggressive, eager, scowling little personality very different from the ingratiating finches, and because of his raucous, scolding voice was called Donald, for the Duck.

By his downy appearance, his yellow gapers, and the slow rate of his development we realized that he was much younger than Che-Wee had been when we got him, and it is really a miracle that he survived. But the leaves were turning before he was even feeding himself and when Will arrived for another stay and pronounced him a red-eyed vireo (many of whom, it is ruefully acknowledged, have ordinary brown eyes —ah, Science!) we knew that he could never make the long migration to South America which is a part of the vireo yearly program. Neither had we the courage to undertake the permanent feeding and care of yet another bird to whom a cage was not natural. So when we returned to New York in October Donald went to live in the big New England Garden aviary at the New York Zoological Park, where he flourishes at the time of writing and where he will doubtless live longer and much higher than in his natural surroundings. Our bird-family was thus restored to its normal complement of Bitsy and Che-Wee.

It was not easy to part with Donald, though. He was as tame as Che-Wee, and though he ate grasshoppers was clean and odorless. While I corrected galley proof on this passage of the book he sat companionably on the lampshade near by and watched. His eyes, though they were not exactly red, were unusually large and brilliant, and he had a very definite sense of play, and would tug sturdily at a string or a flower and allow you to pull him around by it like a puppy with little whimpering, complaining sounds. He loved to have a red clover or a nasturtium on a long stem, or a cabbage leaf, to play with, and would carry it around in his beak and shake and maul and "kill" it, put his foot on it and tear it to pieces, just as he tore up the decapitated grasshoppers he finally learned to handle himself. As his plumage grew he was really beautiful, with a snow white front and olive back and wings, a grey head, and the black stripe through the eyes which gave him a singularly intent, almost cross-eyed stare. His desire for human company was as great as Che-Wee's, and he had a cuddlesome quality all his own, so that he liked to edge inside your collar and sit down next your neck, and he enjoyed a hovering hand over him even when full-grown. Also he developed nightmares, probably due to the migrating instinct, and would wake about midnight and flutter against the bars of his sleeping cage, until carried out into the light and allowed to sit on your hand and have a drink of water and a snack of egg-yolk, when he would again subside, comforted, and sleep till his cage was uncovered in the morning.

I don't advise anyone to go out and look for trouble in the shape of a baby bird to rear, and it is never wise to take them away from a spot where the old birds are trying to look after them. But if they are deserted or unable to fly, there are a few simple rules. Thick bills mean seed-eaters and they can sometimes be saved with hard-boiled egg-yolk and bread and milk, slightly warmed, or better than bread the Canary Egg-biscuit which is a corrective diet for either diarrhea or the other thing. If they are too young to pick it up for themselves the shadow of your hand over their heads or a jarring of the perch where they sit will usually make them open their mouths and you can push it in. Tweezers or forceps help for this. Feed often and not too much at a time. Every hour or so.

A dish of canary seed and song-food with a bit of bird gravel alongside and heads of blue-grass from the edge of the lawn will finally convey the idea of picking if held under their noses and moved around. Water should not be poured down their throats for fear of getting it in their lungs. A bright teaspoon full of water moved back and forth in front of them will attract their attention and finally they will learn to drink.

Thin-billed birds are much more difficult to raise. Small

grasshoppers minus their spikey back legs and hard head parts and papery wings are safest, and the little green measuring worms. Earth worms aren't much good except for robins. Scraped raw beef which has had scalding water poured over it and the Egg-biscuit soaked in warm milk will do as alternative meals. I keep a couple of spare cages now, quite large, with dark covers, and I leave the bird after feeding in the covered cage in a darkened room a good deal of the time. Enforced rest and no opportunity to thrash round and try to fly will help it to mend. I disturb it within every two hours for feeding, oftener if it gets restless. Flying lessons have already been mentioned. Try not to let it land hard or fall down behind things in its attempts—this sometimes requires considerable agility on the part of the foster parent.

As soon as it can feed itself and fly, an insect eater usually has to be turned out to take its chances. They are too difficult in their diet for a year-round pet except in zoological gardens, though meal worms, mocking-bird food and ants' eggs can be procured, and a sort of mash made of egg-yolk, crumbs, and cod-liver oil can be made. A certain amount of hardening is possible if the cage can be kept on a screen porch or in a room with an open window, but not in too low a temperature, and the cage must always be covered at night. Very small birds should be hovered in a box full of fluffed out Kleenex, frequently changed. And make up your mind that it will probably die no matter what you do. If it does, go and buy that canary to comfort you.

A long drought dried up reliable springs in every direction, but ours still ran its overflow half full, though we did less watering of the garden this year than heretofore and the bloom suffered accordingly. To the casual eye it still looked pretty well. The red raspberry and blackberry crop were terrific, and the new strawberry bed was allowed to produce a little fruit at the end of the season. The bed is laid out by Elmer according to the three-year plan approved by a friend of his who does well in the strawberry market. The plants are set two feet apart in rows, and all blooms were removed for weeks. The runners are all snipped off until next year, when one runner will be rooted between the present plants, the latter being allowed to bear all season. The rest of the runners will be removed next year as well. The third year the parent plant is removed and thrown away and the runner bears. And so on.

We had three pints of lovely clear pale honey from the oldest hive, pressed out of the comb which they overbuilt before the super with the box-combs went on, and the first combs are about to be removed from that. The strawberry bed having taken the site of the old vegetable garden, the newly reclaimed space behind the plant house was enclosed in a stout electric fence and trip wire and Elmer planted everything to be grown for the table there. From now on the garden is part of his job, it was too much for us. We bought a baby power-cultivator which does in an hour what it would take a man all day to do with a hoe, in the big new garden behind the plant house, and our three-year-old asparagus bed supplied us for weeks.

We had our own side-delivery rake for haying at last, and Roy and Leon came back for hay week. Because of the record drought there was for once little worry about rain on cut hay, and in spite of the drought our stand of hay was fairly heavy—it was fertilized again last autumn. And the demand for it was such that one truck load of bales was picked up right off the field by the purchaser.

We have come apparently to another turning point. We can sit back as we are, and be solvent and moderately productive, and gradually earn our investment back. Or we can go further and really amount to something as a going concern. When I say that anyone can do what we have done so far, I am not talking through my hat after having spent reckless thousands on reclamation and equipment and labor. I have certainly put as much again into the place as I paid for it. But the results of that modest expenditure are all still here, still in daily use, still worth every penny of it. If further investment would pay off as well, in produce and daily satisfaction, it is only a question of finding the money. But we are not going to ride off madly in all directions.

I still cling stubbornly to the idea of beef cattle, and only the time and the expense of laying out the charged wire fence which must come first stands between me and my desire. As for a cow, I am content to buy and pasteurize milk indefinitely and to use butter out of a box. So far as I can see, a cow is about as much daily trouble as a very small baby without the same compensations either now or later.

Chickens I can practically guarantee. About once a month Elmer and I can be discovered roaming the immediate hinterland of the house and barn with anxious expressions and broad, squarish gestures of the arm—a sure sign that the exact site of the chicken-house and run is again under discussion. It must be most discreetly chosen—not too far from the house, because of the foxes and the weasels, not too near because of the sacred landscape as seen from the house and the barn windows. Only the problem of its location and the expense of building a not unsightly modern home for hens has stood between me and chickens. This can't go on much longer. By next year something is going to pop on chickens. Rhode Island Reds. And maybe that black Angus baby bull for the foreground beyond the strawberry bed. . . . Ten more acres to be reclaimed for hay, by going over the land beyond the sugar-house with the bush-and-bog harrow, fertilizing, and re-seeding—land which for want of regular mowing before we bought it has gone to golden-rod and steeple-bush. And five hundred more young maple trees to be tapped. And half a dozen more beehives, with boxed honey as a sideline to the maple syrup. And a dozen young apple trees set out in the lower meadow for the bees to work on. And the perpetual, judicious thinning of the woods for a straighter, healthier growth of the chosen trees that are left. . . .

In the English style of country house nomenclature we have been advised to call the place Little Veracity. Some people don't think that is a bit funny, but old Wodehouse, *Punch*, and Thirkell readers like ourselves appreciate the finer points. The fact is, it's never going to be called anything, and there will never be a shiny station-wagon with a fancy name painted in green letters on the door.

We are still so far short of what we would like to accomplish and of what we *might* do that I feel a little foolish now about having made what may seem a premature report on progress. But nothing is too little, just as nothing is too much, to do for the land. However slowly you must proceed, whatever it may mean in more obvious and immediate luxuries deferred, it is worth while to do what you can. It may turn out to be more than you think. And in the meantime you have fun. And your values shift a little to the good. And you come a bit unkinked. And finally you may find that you have written another one of those Driven-Back-to-Eden books.

Postscript

IT IS STARTLING to discover that twenty-five years have passed since this book was first published. I seem to be about the same, and so does Elmer, though Will and my mother and Che-Wee are no longer here. But there is "no empty chair," as a lady named Elizabeth Stuart Phelps Ward has advised us, because to love is still to have. Hardly a day has gone by without Will's name being spoken, as though he had just gone, or would soon be arriving again.

With his usual foresight he chose among our long-time friends one about my age, named Florence, who would soon be retiring from her job, to become a neighbor. She agreed that it would be a good idea if she built a cottage in a corner of my hayfield, halfway down the road to the mailbox, and moved the contents of her New Jersey apartment into it. Elmer had already built himself a commodious camp on the hill a mile away from the house, and its design was adapted for Florence's cottage—living room, bedroom, kitchen and bathroom. Will watched its construction with the keenest interest, and even climbed the ladder to its roof to see the shingles go on, as he had never seen a house being built from the cellar-hole up before.

When in 1962 the time came for me to empty the duplex apartment in New York where he and I had lived for more than thirty years, some of its furniture found a home in Florence's cottage, some went to Elmer's camp, and the rest came here, displacing well-worn pieces with things I was fonder of. Will's scientific library—from Topsell to Hakluyt—went to Princeton, many of the other books went to a dealer, and a great many more came here, overflowing the shelves in the barn-room and the house. The porcelains and bronzes and snuff-bottles which had come back to New York with him from his travels round the world settled in on top of the bookshelves and mantlepiece here without apparent surprise, so that his possessions surround me still. And his guns, from rifles to Lugers, went to Elmer.

This book contains the only authorized view of Will Beebe outside his own writings. He left an expressed desire in his own hand that no biography or "Life" of him should be published, as he had already written everything about himself that anybody needed to know. As this volume was already in print at that time, and had been passed by him with an indulgent smile, I have no compunctions about releasing it again for a new audience.

When I first came to Vermont in the early 1940's there had been no talk of "second homes" as a refuge from city violence, there was no forced bussing of school children, there were fewer unsolved crimes of senseless murder and vandalism, and a woman alone could go to the theater at night in New York and travel home by bus or taxi without apprehension. I did it myself, and walked a dog in the city streets after dark without incident. I didn't come to Vermont because I was afraid to live in New York, but because in 1940 we had lost our house in Bermuda to the war and wanted a weekend place for relaxing and entertaining our friends.

I have stayed in Vermont because my husband died and I had to forego the expense and inconvenience of keeping up a large apartment in New York as well as a home in the country which I preferred for the sake of a pet, and I had found running back and forth rather an effort. Now the whole balance of my life has shifted to the country, and as things have turned out in New York I am very thankful, though for me it happened to be just a piece of blind luck.

The old house has acquired picture windows now, and three bathrooms, a combination gas and oil range in the kitchen, an automatic oil burner furnace, a dishwasher, three television sets, a freezer in the barn-room. I have long since learned to drive Elmer's jeep truck and my own easygoing Olds. Company light and power finally arrived through Elmer's diplomatic efforts, and the light-plants were retired, though they can still be hooked up to the house in an emergency. A private telephone line eliminated the stealthy click of receivers being taken down all along the line when my bell rang three times. (A natural perversity always prompted Will, when calling me from New York, to say outrageous things for the benefit of the eavesdroppers, and I was sure they swallowed every word of it, to my intense embarrassment, and his willful delight.)

With Florence as a back-up driver, I made a number of trips to Virginia in the Sixties, while writing four books drawn from the records and correspondence files at Mount Vernon—an experience for me on a level with those in England during my lovely days there before the 1939 war. Mount Vernon was enchantment—a researcher's paradise, the more appreciated because my research there was unique in the traditionally exclusive organization. I had won my spurs in their estimation with a life of Washington (*Potomac Squire*) which is still available in their sales room.

The job necessitated traveling with a typewriter, a tape-recorder, and innumerable notebooks, besides the bulky scripts and carbons and typing paper, and Florence and I always arrived laden like gypsies at the staff parking lot behind the administration building. In order that I might use the evenings for work, we were always privileged to live inside the gates, which were locked at 5 P.M. We would find the central table in the library room cleared and all the surrounding surfaces covered with the box files and records laid out for my use, and everyone else put off for the duration of my stay—a courtesy and indulgence I did my best to repay in a 2-volume history of the Mount Vernon Ladies' Association.

It is my favorite production in a lifetime of writing books, just as the friendships made there with the members of the staff are among my most precious.

At the latest count I have written some thirty-two books, though when and how they all got done I have no idea, as none of the rules for writing books has been followed—except the one so well stated by Red Lewis, about "the application of the seat of the pants to the seat of the chair."

As I read again the account of the first years in this house, I am made very aware of the passing of time, with a dim nostalgia for even the inconveniences of the early wartime years. There have been changes indeed, and not all for the best. The most drastic was perhaps the invasion of the state of Vermont by the ski industry, which resulted in the selling of all available land at boom prices. Taxes rose enormously, along with prices, and there was a rash of new lodges, restaurants, and golf courses, besides an influx of not always desirable strangers in our once quiet village. It made more jobs, of course, and local labor was absorbed at once by the newcomers at higher wages, which was largely responsible for our giving up the sugaring and haying . . . not without regret and a half-promise to ourselves that we hadn't *really* quit.

And there was suddenly less call for hay, after we had risen to owning our own baler, after waiting for rental rigs for years, and we even rented it out ourselves.

The sugar house, weather-tight and tidily put to bed as always, still stands as Elmer habitually left it in the spring. We had even installed a handsome, enviable steam boiler-rig, which did away with the annual woodcutting chore; and it made superb syrup. Wood is now cut only for the little black antique parlor-stove which has been set into the fireplace to save furnace oil in these stringent times.

Finch families still bicker and flutter around the feeders on the porch, though there are no birds inside the house now. For some foolish reason the government has put a ban on the sale of canaries, so that Woolworth's bird cages are reduced to parakeets, which do not appeal to me. I have switched to cocker spaniels, and am now on my third one, a blonde after two black ones. The first was a girl whose kennel name was Melody, which just happened to be the title of a book I was writing when she came to console me for Che-Wee's death. She wasn't young then, but she was small and cuddly, and took life as it came, with dignity and philosophy, but the New York vet couldn't save her from some powerful New York germ. The second spaniel came to console me for Melly's death, which happened between Thanksgiving and Christmas; he was therefore called "Jinglebells," and always had his own little Christmas tree, which he surveyed with grave appreciation from a distance. He was very black and very wise, and lived with all the grace in the world to be sixteen years old.

The house was unbearable without him, but my friend Gladys Taber told me where to find another cocker quick. I believe that if ever you have had room for a pet, you *always* have room for a pet, and should waste no time in mourning, because you owe somebody a home.

Jody, whose second name is Bells, is so blonde and beautiful that people think he is a girl, which embarrasses him, as no one was ever more of a gentleman. When we drove down to Massachusetts to pay a visit to Gladys Taber's friends who raised blue-ribbon spaniels for show, I intended, of course, to get another black one. But Jody was the only male puppy available, and while I was trying to persuade myself that I could make do with his rather pushy little black sister, in Melly's memory, Jody was already sitting in Elmer's lap, confident that he was the One. His pedigree was as long as your arm, and Elmer said he was a Thinker. So I wrote out the check, his papers were signed, and he was put into the car, and on the way home he somehow got himself named Jody.

He must have sensed from the first that he had come to a place where he would be cherished and loved as very few little dogs are lucky enough to be, and he has responded with an obliging good behavior and good humor which very few little dogs achieve. Romping with Elmer and running on a private road and lawn where there is no threat of traffic or kidnapping, he has grown very big for a cocker—too big now for show—and very strong in a tussle. He has a superb coat, and an expression of amiable awareness which is truly devastating, with enormous intelligent eyes and a neat little black nose in the middle of his golden face. Everyone tries to name his color—buff, honey, champagne, golden, jonquil, amber, straw, cream, flaxen, tawny —the adjective contest goes on endlessly, till the thesaurus comes up with *zanthochroid*, from the Greek word for yellow, which reduces everyone to respectful silence.

The small power lawn mower has been superseded by a handsome rider mower type which has enlarged the lawns and which Jinglebells used to ride on in Elmer's lap, his long spaniel ears flying in the breeze. Jingles was slightly deaf, but Jody says the mower is too noisy and hurts his hearing, and he won't go near it when the motor is running. The handsome green John Deere crawler which replaced T-20 for the sugaring is still in use for clearing the barnyard of snow piled up by the town plow after a heavy storm.

The Rhode Island Reds came . . . and are gone. For years we had a busy, prosperous henhouse and gathered, candled, boxed, and sold our own eggs. But as the flock thinned down and aged we didn't renew it. The chicken house, built alongside the plant house behind the hedge, was snug and winterized, but the cold weather confined them too long. We gave the last survivors to a neighboring farmer, to join his flock.

The deer and the bear have withdrawn more deeply into the woods, away from all the building and "developing" which has been going on, and are seldom seen on the lawn or in the nearby field any more. As the house sits well in the middle of its land on a dead-end road our privacy has not been much intruded upon, except by out-of-state "explorers" who don't believe in signs, and must make a shamefaced or impudent turn-around in the barnyard, to the accompaniment of Jody's ferocious barking.

The most noticeable and most depressing change is the growing violence in the world around us, which makes the mild hold-up scare that once drove Che-Wee and me to an overnight refuge in the village seem rather like a picnic. Nowadays, when professional terrorism has become a weapon as dauntless and apparently insoluble as gunpowder once seemed in the 16th century, and the kidnapping and murder of innocent hostages is becoming a frequent news item, one would not treat so lightly the warning that desperate fugitives were at large in the neighborhood. This is presumably Hitler's legacy to the world; on top of the holocaust he perpetrated in the Forties, he brought an end to the easygoing, love-thy-neighbor world my generation grew up in.

There is a new generation now, its nervous system and mentality twisted by lifelong familiarity with brutality and horrors. And yet there are odd contradictions to this impression, such as my fan mail, much of which indicates an obstinate appreciation of a supposedly outgrown thing called Romance. I have always written books with love stories in them—stories which run to a reasonably happy ending, which is no longer stylish. Yet I get no complaints, and am often thanked by people who acknowledge themselves as teenagers, and who want more of the same. I am touched by such naiveté, in this hard-boiled world, and take trouble over my replies—as when a fourteen-year-old girl who wanted to be a fashion designer when she grew up, wrote asking me for a picture and further description of a "blue dress" mentioned in *Yankee Stranger*—as though she expected it to be hanging in my wardrobe. I could only refer her to the *Godey's Lady's Book* files for 1860, where I had seen something at least similar, and I hope her local library could produce a set of *Godey's*.

The very old and the very young are the letter

writers, which is not to say the ones in between never write. But it gives me a real lift of the heart when someone who says she is eighty-some and was raised on family tales of the War Between the States writes me to approve a battle scene in *Yankee Stranger* and to add some local traditions of her own for my amusement. And once a veteran of Corregidor wrote from a military hospital in California to say that he had adopted my Williamsburg family for his own, as he had no near relations at all, and asked questions which showed that in his imagination he had gone on with the story and was living a fantasy life of his invention with the characters I had provided in the book.

Often a quite lively correspondence will arise from my routine reply to a fan letter, which the writers always seem to be surprised to receive. (I once wrote a book, *Letter to a Stranger*, which of course, never happened to me, but which arose out of the unexpected intimacies a reader will confide to a favorite author who has become a kind of imaginary friend.)

Presumably some authors do draw on their own experiences and acquaintances in devising a book—Somerset Maugham was one—and out of this bad habit misunderstandings and lawsuits can arise. But that to me is not real authorship; it is cheating. A story should come out of the air, as a project to be developed from next to nothing, without the crutch of personal experience, and I have spent a good deal of effort explaining this to people who have found a fancied similarity to some experience of their own, though how they suppose I have divined what has happened to them is never mentioned, or why they assume that I have dramatized some event in my own life remains a mystery.

Now, instead of a small brown bird gripping with fragile feet the noisy carriage of my typewriter as it jerks along the page, there is a silent, patient dog asleep in the chair pulled close to the corner of my desk as I write. He knows that eventually it will be tea time, when work will be suspended and he will have his own special Arrowroot biscuit—"Baby's first cookie"—out of his own tin, while "people" eat indigestible things like chocolate cakes, which are not good for dogs. And after that there will be a walk down the road in the afternoon sunshine— never unaccompanied, for he has been royally spoiled and won't set out alone now, and better that he doesn't. Jody's life is secure and serene and on a delightful country routine of naps and meals and walks, and there is always somebody's bed to sleep on the foot of at night if he gets tired of his own basket—and we hope to keep it that way.

—Elswyth Thane
Wilmington, Vermont